# WHEREWOLVES

A Novel by

John Vamvas & Olga Montes

WHEREWOLVES

This is a work of fiction. All characters, organizations, and events portrayed in this novel are either products of the authors' imagination or are used fictitiously. Any resemblance to actual events or locales or persons, living or dead, is entirely, and remarkably, coincidental.

http://wherewolvestheblog.com

Editor: Shelley A. Leedahl
http://www.writersunion.ca/member/shelleya-leedahl

Cover art and design by
Anthony Jones Nestoras

ISBN: 978-0-9918666-1-8

To Daphne and Achilles
who had to put up with us while we
wrote.

And in memory of Leeko
(July 1st, 1996 – July 29th, 2011)

*What is a monster? Something that grows hair all over and howls? Could be. But the real monster is within, and when it comes out, it's as fugly as you see it, or as it lets you see it.*

# TABLE OF CONTENTS

# The Kids

## The Geeks

Doris – A pretty girl with purple-streaked dark hair.

Jeffrey – Doris's best friend.

## The Outcasts

Elie El-Hage – A Lebanese-American with thick, dark hair.

Alex Peterson – Elie's girlfriend. An Eastern-European beauty.

## The Foursome

Zack Schwartz – The actor.

Kimberly Jones – A pretty African-American with long cornrows and marble blue eyes.

Abigail Simmons – A Southern, self-obsessed, strawberry blonde.

Dawn Evans – A quiet Goth girl who always has music plugged into her ears.

**The Putrids**

Jonathan Johnson (J.J.) – Stud quarterback and leader of the pack.

Lance Willis – A 250 lbs African-American football player (Tight-End) with a shaved head.

Scott McCalla – A green-eyed jock known as "The Hooper Hunk".

Cindy Chen (Kitty) – Scott's girlfriend. An Asian-American petite girl with platinum-blonde hair.

Ronald (Obama) Collins – He looks like President Obama.

Heather –A blonde bombshell and Ronald's girlfriend.

George Garcia – "The Latin Pit Bull."

Rosa Ortiz – George's girlfriend.

Billy-Bob Jenkins (Swifty) – Tall and lean with red hair and freckles. Wears roller shoes and spiked boots.

Sharon Jenkins – Billy-Bob's twin sister.

## Chapter 1

## THE ENDING – WEREWOLVES?

Dilly runs. The deafening beat of her panting isn't enough to drown out the monstrous growls and trampling that rumble behind her. Though she can't see well enough to dodge the naked branches slicing into her, the full moon's rays help her find the path. *This way*, the young woman tells herself, and takes a left. *Now right!* Her body veers. She slams her beaten shoulder against the thick trunk of a sugar maple. *Ah, fuck!* The pain electrifies her cells. Like sticking a finger in a thousand volt

1

socket. She falls to one knee. *Don't you fucking stop! Move! Move! Move!* She forces herself up and implores her feet to barrel forward.

*There it is! The fallen stump that looks more like a giant claw!* She makes a mad dash for it, hurtles over the trunk, lands on all fours, and snaps her head back. She gasps, "Yes!" eyes on the nest-like bundle cradled between the two lower branches of the tall yellow birch before her.

She can hear whatever is out there tearing through the brush.

She leans against the tree's peeling, gray bark and kicks at the dead leaves on the ground. *Come on!* she screams in her head. And at last feels the line dig into her ankle. She yanks it back hard. *Click.*

A thunderous roar!

She throws herself to the ground and in the next instant, a burlap sack swooshes over her.

*Slam!*

A canine screech rips through the forest.

Dilly jolts, feels the ground, and snatches a heavy rock. She thrashes her head from side to side and strains to hear the danger, but hears only the sack's long suspended rope creaking as it swings. She gets to her knees. A branch snaps, she spins to pitch the rock— *Nothing's there.* "Breathe, girl,

2

*breathe,*" she reminds herself. And inhales deeply. The prominent scent of balsam firs transports her to the weekend she spent with Brian in a cozy bed and breakfast last May. Her eyes well. *Brian* … She scans the beech, spruce, and birch tree outlines, caressing her ring—its diamond lost to the forest. *We should have never … ahh …* She brushes off tears. *Be strong,* she compels herself. She staggers to a stand and lumbers off.

A harrowing growl booms—her feet are in the air, her face smashes to the ground.

"No! Nooooo!" she screams, as she's dragged across the underbrush.

Pebbles, leaves, and branches cut into her. Her fingernails claw a trail into the earth as she tries to grip at something—anything—that will anchor her long enough to turn over and hurl the rock she still has gripped in her hand. A trio of saplings gashes her chin and she grabs onto them, jerking to a stop.

She fears she'll be rent in two as she's tugged savagely. But she doesn't let go. *I've got to …* She tries to twist—*turn my … fucking arm … over …*

Light shines through from approaching high beams. Distant, but just enough of a distraction. *Yes!*

She whips the rock.

A painful yowl!

"Fuck you!" she bellows as she scrambles to her feet and darts for the auspicious lights. She pushes her way through a thicket of juniper shrubs, waving and hollering—"Hey! Hey!"—and scarcely manages to catch herself. Shafts of light from the oncoming vehicle reveal there is nowhere to go but down. Down a ridiculously steep hill, she discovers.

The charging footsteps close in.

*Shit!* She glances over her shoulder—*Fuck!*—and drops to the ground. She gropes the ridge, clasps a sturdy root, and slides over the edge. Splinters stab into her hands. "Ahhhh!" she squeals—*Shut up!*—and hangs on. She cocks her head east to west. *I need … something … else … to grab on … to.*

The thicket rattles and cracks.

She winces. *No!* The rocks beneath her feet crumble. *Oh my God, oh my God. Don't you fucking let go.* Her feet dangle. The roots dig deeper into her palms. "Ahhhh!" She presses her mouth into the dirt and feels the earth above vibrate. A pebble bounces off her head.

Beastly snorts and growls turn into sniffing and heavy panting.

She holds her breath. *Go away, go away, go away!*

The noises above her suddenly fade; all she hears is an eerie, unsettling breeze.

*Oh my God!* She listens hard. *They're gone. Breathe,* she reminds herself again. She inhales and looks down. The slope is too extreme. She needs another path. She waits a long moment—*God help me!*—takes another mouthful of air, then musters the strength to pull herself up. *Please don't be there. Please don't be there. Please*—Fiery breath steams her forehead, and a snarl swells into a ferocious roar.

Dilly glimpses the blur of black, indigo, royal blue below. And lets go.

*** 

Drew steers the eighteen-wheeler down the unlit, rural highway with his knee. *Goddamn,* he complains, passing an exit on the steep road, *I'd give my left nut for one of Old Man Sam's brownies right now.*

He loves small towns—their diners *respect* truckers—and, besides—he wipes his mouth and tugs at his salt-and-pepper goatee—the Eats All Nite has the most delicious brownies he's ever sunk his crooked teeth into. *Wish I'd made better time,* he thinks. He slips his fingers into his jean jacket's breast pocket and pulls out a cigarette. Lights it—in spite of the thousands of gallons of fuel he's hauling. His other hand fidgets with the radio.

"Fifteen arrests were made at Club Rave On Wednesday night—" He switches the station. "—the two average-sized youths overpowered the burly bouncers—"

*Bouncers, yeah, right. Little girlies.* "Ha! Ha!" He flips the station.

"Police are still searching—" he jabs the button again and catches a favorite song's final verse. "That's right, baby, sing it to me. Let me be your Bobby McGee."

He hums along.

"That was Janis with 'Me and Bobby McGee'. We'll be back with the news right after this."

"News ..." He takes a long drag of his cigarette. "Who gives a shit?" He puffs out a series of rings, one into the other, and reaches for the radio.

*What the—?* He slams on the brakes. "Holy shit!" His stubby fingers squeeze the steering wheel as the truck screeches to a stop.

"Oh my God!" He jumps out of the cab— motor still running—spits out his cigarette, and runs to the shoulder of the road. *Oh, fuck, I killed—* The headlights expose a mangled heap of torn, blood-soaked leather. *I ... I couldn't possibly have ...*

*There's no way I … The truck barely touched* —He leans over —*her.*

Dilly springs up.

Drew jumps back. "Goddamnit! Goddamnit!"

Her bloodshot eyes widen.

"Are you crazy?" he shouts. "What the hell were you doing in the middle—"

Her bruised mouth stretches grotesquely and she belts out an agonized scream. She points at something behind him.

He whirls. Beyond the ditch, the trees and shrubs are being pushed apart. Like curtains after an encore, he thinks. *A fucking bear!* he imagines. "Oh, fuck! Fuck me!" He grabs Dilly and leads her to the passenger door. *It's locked!* "Shit!" He pulls her to his door. "Come on! Come on! Move!" He swings the door open and lifts her by the waist. "Get in! Get in!" A pink thong rises above her black leather pants. *Damn! Of all things,* he thinks.

He jumps in and she scrambles onto the passenger seat.

The radio warns, "If seen, police insist you do not approach. Repeat, do not approach. Call your local authorities immediately." Jimi Hendrix's "Foxy Lady" begins to blare.

Drew locks his door and throws the truck into gear. "Let's get the hell outta here!" He scans his mirrors and windows. *Where is it? Was it a bear?* He switches off the radio and turns to her.

She's trembling and whimpering. She tugs at her deep brown hair, woven with twigs and dead leaves. Hazel eyes shift wildly, streaming mud-lined tears. Full lips dribble blood onto her hot-pink bra—*Wow, she must be one sexy babe under all that.* He shakes off the thought. "You all right?" he asks.

\*\*\*

*Thank God*, she thinks, eyeballing the trucker. Rugged. Beefy. He turns up the cab's heater, and hot air wafts down her open jacket. *Shit.* Her bra is showing, she realizes, and she zips the jacket up to her neck before curling into a ball.

Drew reaches for his cell phone on the dash. "Look," he says softly, "I'm going to call—" A scraping sound—loud and discomforting, like a nail etching glass—grinds into his left ear. His back teeth rattle. "Jesus!" He leans into his smeared window. "What the—"

Dilly strains to see. *Mud—blood! Oh, fuck!*

A shrill growl blares!

He jerks back.

Another growl!

She screams and jumps out of her seat. "It's on my side, too!" She points to her smeared window

8

and grabs on to his arm. Doors rattle, as though being yanked by strong, unseen hands. The scraping escalates. Ear-pounding metal hammers, threatening to deafen.

"Oh, yeah?" he yells, laying into the pedal. "Let's see if they can hang on to *this*." He swerves down the black highway.

Dilly squints. She sees something ahead. "Look," she points at a sign. "Next exit. Hope, 27 miles. We'll never make it!" she cries.

***

Drew is aware of her clutching fingers through his thick jacket. "Hang on, sweetie. This fucker's getting off."

"You're going to get us killed!" she yells.

"Not *us*, baby!" He veers close to the sign and the cab momentarily buckles as the side fender smashes into it. "Yes!" he yells, and takes a deep breath. He turns to deal with what's on his left. "I can't see through that shit." He switches on the exterior LED lights, transforming the truck into a runaway carnival ride. Then feels under his seat for his crowbar. He turns to her. "What the hell was—?" She's still shivering, he notes. "You okay, honey?" he asks. She just sits there, gnawing her thumbnail. "Look, I'm going to have to roll down my window a bit," he says.

"No, no, please, *please* don't!" She recoils.

"It's okay." He holds up the crowbar. "Just a quick check. You go up there, behind me." He indicates with his chin. "In the sleeper."

He places his knee under the steering wheel, raises the crowbar in his right, and with his shaky left hand, clutches the handle. Inch by inch he lowers the window. "Nothing but cornfields," he says, "They're gone." The truck slows as it chugs up a steep hill. Drew casts a glance at the top bunk; the woman's huddled under the sleeping bag. He's surprised by her agility. *Fuck, did she get up there fast. Must be in shock,* he thinks. *Man, is she gonna feel all her shit later.* He grabs his phone.

The operator answers. "911, what's your emergency?"

"Yes, hello. I've got a woman here who's been seriously injured, she's been scratched, bitten and—"

"Sir, where are you calling from?"

"I'm in my truck on the Thirteen South about twenty-seven miles from Hope—"

BAM! BAM! The top of the cab rattles.

"Oh shit!" Drew cries.

Dilly jumps from the bunk and—legs tangled in the sleeping bag—smashes into his right arm. His phone drops to his feet.

10

BANG! BANG! BANG!

She screams.

GROWLLL …!

She screams again, and claws to get as near the trucker as possible.

"Sir? Sir?" the voice of the 911 operator echoes from the receiver.

"Lady, please!" Drew pushes the hysterical woman off him. "I can't steer!" He reaches for his cell phone. The truck hits a bump and lifts him off his seat. His foot comes down hard, crushing the phone. "Fuck!"

Pounding, scraping and growling swaddle the cab.

"Oh, please, God, I don't want to die." Dilly crouches between the two seats, and weeps.

"Don't worry, lady," he assures her, as the truck crests the hill and starts gathering speed, "I got 'em exactly where I want. Sit down! Fasten your seat belt!"

Dilly kicks off the sleeping bag, clambers back into her seat, and fumbles with the safety belt in between sobs.

"Shhh." Drew hisses. "Listen."

Dilly glances from window to window. "I don't hear anything," she says over the dull hum of the truck.

"Exactly. They're gone," he murmurs, lifting his cap and wiping the sweat from his brow.

"I-I-I don't think so," she stutters, and begins to chew on her nail again.

"Yeah ... I'm going too fast." He points at the speedometer. "They must've fallen—"

KNOCK, KNOCK, KNOCK on the passenger door. He turns to the young woman.

She sits, frozen. He watches her eyes bulge. She swallows as if her throat were tightening. She points. "Look out!"

CRASH! The windshield shatters.

"SON OF A BITCH!" Drew floors it. "HOLD ON!" he hollers, trying to see through the fragmented glass. The truck races down the hill. He grips the handbrake lever, sees the speedometer at 90 mph. *Wait, wait, wait ...* Needle hits 100. *Now!* He pulls the lever then pushes it back in again. The truck screeches and jerks violently.

"We're going to die!" The seat belt cuts into Dilly's collarbone.

"Uh-uh." He grabs the crowbar and smashes the windshield out. Ice-cold wind storms the cab. He fights to keep the rig between the yellow lines. *Easy, girl, easy.* "Just gotta ... straighten her ... out .... Goddaaaaamn!" he rejoices as he takes control of the vehicle. He leans out the front and swings

12

the crowbar overhead to probe for danger. *Nothing's there.* He turns to her. "Roll down your window."

She digs her fingers into her seat, quivering wildly.

"Roll it down!" he shouts over the fury. "Don't worry, I got you covered."

She shakes her head and curls into a ball again.

"You don't roll that window down," Drew tells her, "I'm gonna have to stop and go on out there."

She leans away from the window and rolls it open with her fingertips.

"Thank you," he says.

In the cracked wide-angle mirror: two dark figures diminish into the night.

"What the hell are they?" he asks.

She offers a vacuous stare.

Eyes back on the road, the full moon catches his attention. He gazes at it, and gulps a mouthful of bitter air. *Naaaah!* he tells himself, and turns his focus back at his shuddering passenger. *You're lucky I didn't stop for that brownie, sweetie,* he thinks. He spots the sleeping bag between the seats and lifts it to her. She reaches for it. Their hands meet.

He takes hers into his. "Drew's the name. Drew Daniels".

She presses his yellow-stained fingers to her lips. "Thank you."

He cups her cheek gently, then glimpses the rearview. "Oh, no!" He unclamps the fire extinguisher latched onto the left side of his seat.

*** 

On the shoulder of the road, Drew battles the flames searing his rear tires. "Get out of the truck!" He hollers. "Lady! Get out of the—" Wind gushes. The extinguisher powder burns his eyes and shoots into his lungs. He chokes and coughs, yet squeezes the canister for all it's worth. A sudden flash of red, white and blue bounces off the mountainside. He rubs his eyes. "It's about time!" he croaks over his rumbling engine. Emergency, state trooper, and reporter vehicles approach from both ends of the highway.

A paramedic races over with an extinguisher, while another tugs Drew away.

"Had to pull ... emergency brake ... must have overheated," he wheezes.

The EMT tries to strap an oxygen mask over Drew's face.

"I'm ... okay," he pants, throat raw. "I'm ... okay. Get the ... lady—" he doubles over "—in ...

14

the—" The paramedic fastens the oxygen mask. Drew pulls it off. "I said, I'm okay!" He chokes on his words. "The lady … get the lady … she's in the cab!" He pushes the young medic toward the truck.

State Trooper Floyd Anderson hurries over. "Sir, you need to remain calm." He secures Drew's mask.

Drew takes in a lungful of pure oxygen then pulls off the mask. "Calm … I *am* calm. What the hell … is wrong with you guys?" He takes a deep breath and wheezes. "Some fucking animals … tried to kill us—" he coughs "—and all you want to do … is put this fucking thing on me!" He flings the mask to the ground.

Anderson smoothly picks it up and presses it against Drew's face again. "What kind of animals, sir?" he says in a soothing tone, sliding the mask's elastic fastener behind Drew's head.

"I don't know—" Drew takes a step back and snaps the mask down under his chin. "The kind that hang on and bang on … your fucking truck," he rasps, then breaks into a coughing fit. He cups the mask over his mouth, gulping for air. He looks up at Anderson with tear-streaked eyes. "The kind that can do *that*," he barely manages to utter, and points an elbow at his semi: door pushed in like a tin can—handle broken off—window—bloody—

muddy—*scraped as if knives chiseled it*, he thinks—antenna snapped off—LED lights crushed—dents all over. "Oh, fuck!" Drew cries. "Look what they did to my truck!"

"Jesus Christ!" Anderson gasps. "Which way did they go?"

"I don't know. I lost them about ... ten miles back that way." He points down the road.

Anderson runs to his vehicle.

"Not too far from a smashed up road sign ... A couple of miles south of it." Drew hisses and inhales another lungful of pure air.

Anderson peels off. Drew turns his attention to the sound of another siren. A trooper vehicle comes speeding down the road and zooms past, following close behind Anderson.

Drew breathes in the clean oxygen and catches sight of the paramedic walking toward him.

"There's no one in your truck, sir," the EMT calls out.

Drew tears off the mask. "What? What the hell are you talking about?" He darts over to the eighteen-wheeler. Looks in, out, scans the trees, circles the truck. "Where the fuck did she go?" he shouts.

16

State Troopers and reporters converge toward him. *Like a goddamn pack of wolves*, he thinks.

\*\*\*

At the Eats All Nite, a vintage television set hangs over Old Man Sam's open kitchen. The TV's sound is overwhelmed by the hydraulic din that emanates from Gary's reefer trailer parked outside. Gary, a regular, sits in one of the twelve once-white booths, ready to dig into a colossal brownie dessert. A couple of artsy college kids, Kurt and Annie, sit behind him cupping tepid coffee mugs.

Kurt frowns at the giant logo on Gary's noisy trailer. "Pirate Pete's Fish and Seafood," he mutters under his breath.

"What?" Annie says, and looks out the bay window too. "Fish?" She sniffs the air over her shoulder. "No kidding."

Old Man Sam makes his way back behind the counter and smiles up at the Blue Ribbons that line the otherwise faded walls—prizes awarded to the brownie recipe.

Gary wags his fork at the television. "Turn it up! Turn it up!" he demands.

Old Man Sam startles and reaches to turn up the volume. "Hey, isn't that your trucker buddy, Drew?"

"Shhhhh," Gary jumps out of his seat.

A special bulletin has interrupted the late night news; a female reporter interviews Drew standing next to his beaten semi.

"Mr. Daniels, what happened out there?" she asks.

Drew shrugs and raises his palms.

"What happened to your passenger?"

"They must have taken her," Drew responds, rubbing the back of his neck.

"Who? Who has taken her?"

"I ah … I don't …"

"Mr. Daniels, what is out there?"

"I don't know. But whatever it is, you come across it … you'd better run for your life."

The bells on the diner door ring. The diner vibrates with the hum of the reefer.

Everyone turns to the sound.

*** 

Trooper Anderson hurries out of his car. Fellow man-in-blue, Trooper Chris Valenza, pulls up behind him and hastens out of his vehicle.

"There." Anderson points his light at the shoulder of the road. "More blood."

Valenza runs over but stops abruptly, whips around, and flashes his light into the trees across the road.

"What is it?" asks Anderson.

"Heard something."

Trooper Anderson also zigzags his light across the road. Both examine the darkness and see nothing but the flashing red, white and blues bouncing off the mountainside.

"I don't see anything." Anderson turns and continues to follow the blood trail.

Valenza keeps his light on the trees.

Anderson whistles between his teeth. "I've got something here."

Valenza takes a step toward him. Again he stops, and snaps his head back. "There's something out there."

"Shhhhh!" Anderson commands. "Look! More blood." His light finds broken, bloody and squashed corn stems. Both officers raise their flashlights: trampled stalks form a path that seems to lead to the neon sign up ahead, EATS ALL NITE – 24 HRS.

"Old Man Sam's!" Anderson sprints toward his vehicle. "Go, go, go!" he hollers. "I'll radio it in." He jumps into his car and peels off.

Valenza is about to open his door when he distinctly hears branches snap.

\*\*\*

The parking lot at the Eats All Nite diner is teeming. Two deputies and four troopers take

19

cover behind their vehicles, guns pointed at every angle of the eatery. Four emergency technicians stand by, clutching equipment bags. Behind the blockade, a handful of reporters hurry to set up their lights, mikes, and cameras.

Trooper Anderson peers through binoculars, past the burgundy Mazda parked by the entrance. Although the front and sides of the modular diner are almost entirely lined with windows, they are covered either by drawn shades or by gobs of thick blood. "I can't see a damn thing," he tells the Sheriff, standing next to him, and also peering through binoculars.

"I'm calling inside," the Sheriff stammers. He punches in the diner's number and points at the blaring fifty-three foot reefer trailer attached to a gold Freightliner that's parked alongside the diner. "Turn that blasted thing off!" he orders a rookie deputy.

A black SWAT van pulls into the lot. A team of four—fully armed—and their Commander scatter and circle the establishment.

The SWAT Commander marches up to the Sheriff. "What do we got, Hank?"

"So far, nothing," the Sheriff replies, holding up his phone, "they won't pick up."

Trooper Anderson's phone rings. "Anderson," he answers.

The Commander pats Hank on the arm and bustles over to his two sharpshooters, who each position and load their sniper rifles on the hood of the Sheriff's car. "What do we got?" he asks them.

They peer into the diner through night vision riflescopes. "It's a goddamned mess, Commander," belts the veteran sharpshooter. "One's barely moving, two others are motionless but appear to be alive, one's scattered all over the fucking place, or maybe it's two, and two—"

Trooper Anderson dashes over, hollering, "You need to hear this!" He hands the SWAT Commander his phone. "It's Trooper Valenza."

"Go ahead," the Commander says into the receiver. He listens. His forehead wrinkles, and he nods. "Copy that." He hands Anderson back his phone and takes out a pair of night vision binoculars from his utility pack. "I'll get an eye inside the diner now," he says. The others freeze. The leader focuses, then— "Shit!" He digs back into the pack and takes out a box of ammunition. "Here," he orders the marksmen, handing them each silver tipped bullets.

"Commander?" they both say with the same questioning look on their faces.

21

Huddled under a table, Kurt and Annie are trembling. Blood oozes down the curtains, windows, and ribbon-lined walls. *Like thick fudge on fresh brownies,* Kurt thinks. Old Man Sam lays in a pool of it. Body parts—arms, legs, head—occupy tables, chairs, and stools. *The gun,* Kurt almost says out loud, *if I can only—*

Annie snivels suddenly.

He turns and looks into his girlfriend's tearing eyes. Her lips begin to quiver.

"They're g-g-going t-t-to kill us, t-too," she whimpers. "You-you-you-you've got to … d-d-do something—"

Deep guttural snarls resonate.

Annie winces.

Kurt starts. *Oh, shit! They heard her.*

Annie grabs at her chest. She opens her mouth as if to speak but begins to gasp uncontrollably.

*She's hyperventilating!* "Annie!" Kurt cries, shaking her. "Annie!" He steals a glance at the gun on the floor. And dives for it.

\*\*\*

"Now! Take them out now!" The SWAT Commander yells.

Two silver tipped bullets shatter the blood-imbrued windows.

## Chapter 2

# THE BEGINNING - EVERYTHING IS HUNKY-DORIS

Doris Mitchell walks. It's a beautiful autumn morning, yet, as usual, she dreads every step that takes her closer to the two story brick building: Hooper High School. She pulls open the door—its weight, a thousand pounds of barred steel. *My prison*, she thinks. She catches a glimpse of herself in the door's glass rectangle, brushes her shoulder length brown hair out of her jacket collar, and tucks her violet-streaked bangs behind her ear. *Everything*

23

*is hunky-Doris* — her daddy used to say that. She rolls her turtleneck up over her studded choker. Squeezes her barbed bracelets; stabbing into her palm. *Feels good*, she moans, pulling her sleeves over them. And steps inside. The bright fluorescents bounce off the loud green walls, penetrating her senses. Spiraling to her pelvis. Like a garden rake grating the soul. She passes a row of open lockers, papers spilling out. *Smells like pain*, she thinks. *Like pain, hormones, and rotting luncheon meat.* She looks down the narrow hallway. *Oh, Daddy, why did you leave me here?*

The only child of a career army soldier, she's been shuffled from place to place — wherever in God's green earth the Army sent him. And although many of her peers share her experience, she feels very much the outsider. *Why don't they like me?* she wonders, methodically stuffing her cell phone's earbuds into her ears. *Maybe because I can't stand their hip hop crap and poopin' pop. Give me C.C.R., Warren Zevon* — her daddy's music — *or even fucking Duran Duran.* She snatches her phone from the belt of her crinoline skirt — *well … maybe one song*, she confesses — and cranks up the volume. Shakira's "She Wolf" — *The only pop that's hop.* She moves to the music and lets it groove her down the hall.

"Geek!" A girl pokes her.

"Freak!" A boy tries to jab her with a pen.

A crumpled piece of paper smacks her in the face.

"Dora the whora." A group of five teens chants.

Doris lowers her eyes and slows her pace. *But it wasn't my fault! He forced me!* She digs her sharp wristbands into her thighs. *Owww! Grrrrr … I wish they would die.* Her feet count the yellow diamonds set against the glistening gray tiles. "Awooooo," Shakira howls. The note courses through Doris's body and she howls along in her head. Werewolves. God, she loves them. And maybe *that's* it. Maybe it's her fascination with werewolves they don't like—images of the hairy beasts *are* plastered inside her locker, and she's drawn one on the toe of her purple Converse high tops, and yet another beams off a patch she's sewn to her backpack. *Whatever*, she thinks. *I'm a senior. This is the last year I'll have to worry about being in this hellhole.* She dances unwittingly. The music blares so loudly, Cindy Chen and Rosa Ortiz's insults go unheard even though they follow almost on Doris's heels. A gust of hot air tickles her nape. She peeps behind: Cindy and Rosa's faces seem like five-foot high grotesquely smiling clown heads. Feeling like

25

they've caught her stepping out of the shower, Doris hastens to her locker.

Doris fumbles with her lock but keeps one eye on Rosa and Cindy, who meet up with their boyfriends across the corridor. *Look at them all, laughing at* me? *They need to look at themselves ... all trendy chic ... you might look great on the outside, but* inside? *Putrid. Disgusting.*

George Garcia rubs his buzz cut, growls, and flexes his bulky body in the 'Most Muscular' pose, ready to grapple with Scott McCalla, the 'Hooper Hunk'—*blessed with the most astonishing green eyes I've ever seen.* Emerald.

"Grrr, I'm gonna *tapa* your ass, bitch!" Scott says.

"The only thing you can do is *besa mi culo, puto,*" George shoots back, pointing at his butt.

Rosa swings her curvy hips: "A fight! A fight! A Latino and a white!" she cheers, and blows George a kiss.

Cindy roots for her boyfriend, Scott. "Get him, baby!" she snarls.

Scott charges at George.

George dodges left. "Too slow, ho." He dances around.

"Oh, yeah?" Scott says.

"Yeah," George taunts. "Come on! You think you can take The Latin Pit Bull? Grrr! Check this out, *cabrón*." George tries a double leg takedown.

But Scott is too fast; he scoops George up and pins him against his locker. "Champion!" Scott shouts, raising his arms, dropping George to his knees.

"Nice move, bro," George says, getting to his feet.

They high-five each other, just missing Ronald's head.

Ronald Collins, a.k.a. Obama—because of his uncanny resemblance to the President—has his girl, Heather Williams, up against her locker and is moving in for a kiss.

The blonde beauty lifts a finger to his lips. "Not in front of the children, please!" She squirms away.

*Cockteaser*, Doris thinks. Ronald chases after Heather like a puppy—*President? Yeah, right! He can't even get laid.* She turns and catches Scott's reptilian leer. She gasps and darts her eyes away, finding: *My friend.*

Jeffrey Dalton, Doris's one friend, does not have the comfort of music. He shuffles down the hall, head bowed, wire-rimmed glasses clinging to the tip of his nose, tattered green hoodie hanging loosely.

Stud Quarterback Jonathan (J.J.) Johnson walks behind Jeffrey, ramming a football up his butt.

"You think it fits?" Jonathan asks Lance Willis, who walks alongside him.

"Sideways!" the Hooper Hawks' humongous Tight End replies. "You know."

*Why don't they leave him alone?* Doris wonders. *Oh, no! Here comes the shit disturber.* She groans.

Billy Bob (Swifty) Jenkins zooms down the hall on roller shoes, cutting over, under and through knapsacks, books, and people. "J.J.! Lance!" he shouts.

Jonathan and Lance spin around, "Swifty!" They high-five him as he rolls between them, bumping Jeffrey, knocking him down.

"Asshole," Doris mutters under her breath, and tries to shield herself with her locker door, her back to the crowd.

"Going long!" Billy Bob yells, raising his hands to catch the football.

Jonathan pulls back the ball and zeros in on Billy Bob's bouncing ginger locks as he zigzags around the crowd. Jonathan scopes for his pass.

Billy Bob dashes over to Doris and lifts her skirt.

Doris whips around, catching Scott mouth, "Fuck!"—he likes what he just saw. His girlfriend, Cindy, punches his arm.

Doris holds down her skirt, her face gone from ashen to scarlet. "Don't do that!"

"Wasn't me, was the wind." Billy Bob grins, makes a three-sixty, jumps, and catches the football. "Touchdown!"

Doris crouches to pick up her books and phone. She looks at Jeffrey for comfort. He drops his eyes and collects what spilled out of his knapsack: sketchbook, textbooks, pencils, and blue thermal lunch bag.

Rosa and Heather singsong, "Doris wears a thong! Doris wears a thong!" They close in on her.

She's cornered. *Don't let them get to you. Don't let them*—

"Check her out, Heather, she's gone *tomate rojo*," Rosa says.

"You don't have to get blush. We all got one on," Heather reaches and snaps Rosa's *tanga*, "See."

"But you, you are so spanky, *mami chula*. Let's check out that *culo* again." Rosa tries to lift Doris's skirt but Doris holds it down tight.

29

"Don't be shy, baby." Heather brushes Doris's bangs to the side of her face and glides a finger over her dark eyebrows. Black-penciled eyes. "You got it, flaunt it. Why, you got that Sasha Grey thing going."

"Sasha who?" Rosa asks.

"Sasha Grey, you know 'the model' from *Entourage*," Heather gestures oral sex. "Yeah, baby," Heather keeps going, "Why, you could pose for *Playboy*."

"No, *Penthouse*," Rosa says.

"No, *Swank*," Heather says.

"Try *Skank*," Cindy snaps, eyeballing Scott.

"I know, I know," Ronald teases, "with that pale tail she can pose for *Fangoria*'s zombie booty of the month."

"I thought you liked them white, Obama," says George.

"Yeah, white but tight and outta fucking sight." Heather juts her butt out and slaps it hard, "Spanky, baby," she purrs.

Ronald tries to grab Heather but bumps into the next teen to walk down the hall: Dawn Evans. "Speaking of zombies, hey, Dawn," he makes and moans like a zombie, "Dawn of the Dead."

Doris watches the girl closely. She hides behind dark clothes, too much dark make-up, and seems to possess a fragile melancholy. *An enigma, this one*, Doris thinks. A teacher once remarked in class that Dawn had the countenance of a toy poodle—unruly black hair falling over huge dark eyes—that's been kicked one too many times. *I guess that's why The Putrids are not so hard on her*, Doris muses. *They must feel sorry for her.* She watches Dawn smile up at Ronald. *Probably can't hear him over the music blaring into her ears*, Doris guesses. She hears her own name again.

"Doris has one on. Do you have one on?" Heather asks Dawn.

Dawn stares blankly.

Heather gently pulls off one of Dawn's earphones. "A thong, baby," she says, snapping her own.

Dawn covers her face with both hands, and scurries off.

Scott snakes through the crowd and moves in. *Oh fuck*, Doris steps back and smashes into a locker. She's caught in his green eyes. *Hypnotic*, she thinks. He puts a hand up on the metal, leans in, reaches under her turtleneck and seizes her collar. "Woof-woof," he says, pulling her ear to his lips. "I want that ass," he whispers. "You sexy bitch." Scott shoots her a wink and swaggers off.

Though she'd never admit it, she feels strangely flattered. The six foot two, blond, strapping jock is, after all, breathtaking.

Cindy jumps in and slaps Doris hard across the face. *What the hell!* Doris is stunned.

Jeffrey runs toward Doris. "Hey, leave her alone!" he yells. Cindy pushes past him and goes after Scott.

Jonathan grabs Jeffrey by his hoodie, pins him against the lockers and drives a hard punch to his stomach. George hurdles over and kicks, just missing Jeffrey's head. Scott pushes away a livid Cindy, dives in, and fakes karate chops to Jeffrey's face, gut and neck before smacking him in the head.

"Is that your girlfriend, freak?" Jonathan demands, his face just inches above Jeffrey's. "Repeat, is that your girlfriend?"

Jeffrey shakes his head.

"Then mind your own fucking business, geek." Jonathan yanks Jeffrey's thick black sideburns.

"Oww!" Jeffrey cries out, cupping the side of his face.

"Is there a problem here?" a commanding voice echoes.

***

Tall, dark, and—as he likes to think—chiseled like G.I. Joe, Sergeant Tim O'Sullivan steps out of his classroom. *What is it now?* he thinks. The imposing teacher—an Iraq War vet—has devised a newly introduced specialized program meant to inspire future recruits. Forever in army fatigues, the forty-four year old leans into his cane—a prop required since a bullet lodged in his right leg—and peers at the students.

"Sir, yes, sir," Jonathan answers, "Geek-freak here was showing aggression, sir."

"Watch your mouth, Johnson," O'Sullivan snaps. "Is that true, Dalton?" he asks Jeffrey.

Jeffrey raises his eyes to the teacher.

The teacher waits for something, anything. Even a "fuck you" would do. But Jeffrey's expression is vacant. *As usual*, the vet thinks.

The bell rings.

"Sir, Doris mooned us, sir," Billy Bob yells over the clamor.

"Get your ass in class," O'Sullivan commands, then grabs the football from Billy Bob. "All of you," he shoves the ball into Jonathan's gut.

The snickering gang breaks up and heads for the classroom.

33

The teacher stands at the door, waiting for the rest. "Come on, move it."

Scott saunters over to Cindy and puts an arm around the petite blonde. She claws it away. He grabs into her platinum bob, glares into her seething, narrow eyes and blurts, "I told you! I told her, like you said, that she's a skank, with a skanky ass. That's all, Kitty." Cindy's eyes soften and she buries her head into the crook of his arm. Scott shoots his teacher a wink in passing as they enter the classroom.

O'Sullivan studies Jeffrey and Doris, still at their lockers, and scratches his graying temples. *What am I going to do with you two?* He is about to speak but decides to give them a moment. He shifts his weight from the cane and limps back into the classroom.

\*\*\*

Jeffrey presses his forehead into his locker's top shelf. He rubs the side of his face. *Oww.* He whines. *Shut up, wimp,* he tells himself. *They* are *right. You* are *a geek-freak. Coward. You have no balls.* He examines the mini movie posters wallpapered to his locker door and stops on *The Wolfman. If only I could be you, I'd—*

"You know, you could have said you were my boyfriend," Doris says wryly.

34

Jeffrey feels his heart in his throat. *I wish,* he thinks, marveled by her dark purple lips. "But I'm not," he says, averting his eyes, fixing them instead on the crowd of werewolf posters, drawings and magazine cutouts taped inside her adjacent locker—a comfort they both share.

"It might have saved you the humiliation." She pulls out a textbook and a sketchpad.

"I doubt it." Books in hand, he hooks the combination lock and spins it closed.

"I hate them." She flings her knapsack into her locker. "All of them. I wish I could— ugghh!" She slams her locker door. Hard.

Chapter 3

# WHO'S YOUR WORST ENEMY?

The familiar echo of vibrating metal travels into O'Sullivan's classroom. As students get to their chairs, the teacher sits at his tidy desk checking off names against a stack of permission slips.

Dawn is seated in the back left corner, furthest desk from the entrance. She peeks through spread fingers past Billy Bob—who's leaning over his desk and fidgeting with the empty chair in front of his— *What's he up to this time?* she wonders—and reads the writing on the board. "The 8 Simple Rules for Survival." She reads each one carefully.

S - Size up the situation, surroundings, physical condition, equipment.

U - Use all your senses.

R - Remember where you are.

V - Vanquish fear and panic.

I - Improvise and improve.

V - Value living.

A - Act like the natives.

L - Live by your wits.

Dawn reads S once again then scans the mostly bare, faded-yellow concrete walls to the larger-than-usual American flag that hangs listlessly off a pole near the entrance. *Surroundings, surroundings,* she repeats in her head, *physical condition.* She stops on Cindy, at her desk in the front corner by the door. *A porcelain doll.* That's what the delicate Asian reminds her of. Dawn used to play with such a doll when her parents were stationed in South Korea—though Cindy's features seem more exotic and kittenesque, thanks to the blonde hair inherited from her mother—Dawn has noticed the family photo taped in Cindy's locker. Fingers still spread over her eyes, Dawn begins to picture her doll with platinum locks.

Cindy whips around and catches Dawn staring.

Dawn starts, *Oh-oh*, and shifts away her attention. She skims her eyes over the desks behind Cindy, spying Ronald leaning across the aisle running his hand up Heather's thigh. Dawn blushes and turns her sights to the flawless Southern strawberry blonde belle, Abigail Simmons—as usual scrutinizing the photos she takes of herself with her phone. Dawn stops a moment to admire the stunning Kimberly Jones's smooth, dark skin set against marble blue eyes. *So pretty*, Dawn thinks. Though Kimberly's fingers text wildly, Dawn catches the glint of her nail polish that matches her eyes. Sitting across from Kimberly, Rosa reads a text off her phone and enthusiastically texts back. Kimberly looks down at her phone, laughs, and texts again. Dawn knows they're texting one another, *I wonder what they're talking about?* George stretches up in his chair to peek over Kimberly's long cornrows, and leans across the aisle to steal a look at his girlfriend, Rosa's, phone. *He must be wondering too*, Dawn smiles to herself and takes a gander over her shoulder at Elie, who's crammed into one of the two desks nudged against the back wall. He studies the *Warrior Ethos and Soldier Combat Skills*

*Handbook*—his thick dark unibrow furrowed atop penetrating black eyes. *Whoa, so intense,* Dawn thinks. The high cheek-boned, bright-eyed brunette in the neighboring desk, Alex Peterson, leans toward him and utters something under her breath. Elie's olive cheeks flush and the mustache above his short-boxed beard stretches to uncover a grin. Dawn can't help but smile too. *What a nice couple.* Her fingers relax and withdraw to the sides of her face.

Alex notices and smiles warmly at her.

Elie glances over at Dawn, too.

Instantly, she draws the blinds that are her fingers once again, leaving just enough space to focus instead on Sharon, at the desk next to hers.

Dawn examines Sharon's pretty face, searching for the differences between the girl and her twin brother, Billy Bob. Alabaster skin tinted with specks of orange. Bright green eyes that haven't yet decided if they want to be blue. Smooth pixie nose. Somewhat pouty lips. Her ginger hair is tied in a loose ponytail—the stray strands seem to dance around her face. *If not for the long hair,* Dawn decides, *Sharon could be mistaken for her brother.* The most noticeable distinction, though, is in the eyes. His usually bare a playful twinkle. Hers reveal kindness and intelligence, Dawn thinks, and betray a painful longing every time she sets her eyes on Jonathan. Jonathan Johnson. The tall, athletic boy with the pale, pointed face and stone grey eyes. *Hot, but too angry*, Dawn determines.

She catches Sharon peering past the empty desk in front of her. The redhead tilts her body to see behind Lance's large, chocolate brown shaved head. *So perfectly round!* Dawn is surprised to notice. Sharon sighs when she beholds Jonathan turn in his seat and flip his chestnut bangs. He chats with Lance—oblivious to Sharon's gaping.

"A thong?" Kimberly blurts out.

Rosa nods emphatically.

Dawn notices Abigail jolt out of her selfie-obsession. The manicured, cleavage-revealing strawberry blond says—in her distinctive Southern drawl—"Doris?"

"Yeah," Kimberly mocks.

The girls break into waves of laughter. Dawn prickles at Kimberly's high-pitched chirp, which is overpowered by Abigail's snorts.

"Simmons, Jones, what's so funny?" O'Sullivan asks, not bothering to lift his eyes from his papers.

"Sir, nothing, sir," Abigail and Kimberly respond—yet they struggle to contain their sniggering when Doris and Jeffrey lumber in.

40

\*\*\*

*Yeah, yeah, that's right, laugh, Putrids,* Doris tells herself and tries her best to ignore the girls. She can't help but steal a peek over her shoulder, though, and instead catches Scott blowing her a gentle kiss. She jerks her head back and catches Jonathan shoot a foot out. "Jeffr—," she warns, as she steps over it—but too late. Jeffrey trips over Jonathan's foot, smashing his chin into her elbow.

Chirps of giggles cease when O'Sullivan raises his head and locks in on Jonathan. "Are you all right, Dalton?"

Jeffrey pushes his glasses back up the bridge of his nose and nods. He turns to Doris, "Sorry," he whispers, and sits at his desk.

Doris is about to slide into her seat behind Jeffrey but spots a thumbtack on her chair.

"Mitchell, sit! You're late," O'Sullivan commands.

She complies, brushing the thumbtack off her seat.

Behind her, Billy Bob leans forward and whispers aloud, "Such a nice ass, I just wanted to pinch it."

Lance guffaws and everyone turns to him. He picks up the thumbtack. "He just wanted to pinch it," he repeats, pointing at Doris.

Her eyes well. *Fucking putrids.* She flips open her sketchpad and begins a fervent zigzagging over the page.

"Oh, poor her. Doris, what's *thong* with you?" Kimberly ridicules.

The class explodes into laughter.

\*\*\*

*Aww, that's not nice*, Dawn thinks, peeking through her fingers.

"All right, all right, you bunch of misfits, settle down." The teacher stands. "First things first: Permission slips." He glides deftly down the aisle in spite of his cane and stands over Lance.

"Willis?" O'Sullivan asks.

Dawn reads the white lettering on the back of Lance's blue football shirt, *Bennett*, she says in her head, *who's Bennet?* Lance's body quakes. *He's still laughing*, she sees. *He's so mean!*

"Giants or Jets, son?"

Lance pats the number eighty-five on his shirt. "Sir, Giants all the way, sir!" he yells.

"Slip?"

Lance hands him the permission slip and the teacher continues down the aisle.

"Jenkins!"

Sharon and Billy Bob both hold out their slips. As O'Sullivan takes them, Zack Schwartz, the narcissistic self-appointed movie star, waltzes into the classroom.

"Sir, I'm sorry," Zack apologizes, flashing his dazzling teeth. "Rehearsals ran late last night, sir." He slips into his seat behind Lance, and fluffs his black quiff. *He's so cute*, Dawn sighs.

Zack's phone goes off. The ringer tone is a woman's orgasmic cries. The class erupts once again. Dawn feels her cheeks flush.

"Shhhh." O'Sullivan holds up his hands.

"Sir, sorry," Zack quickly turns off his phone. "The GF misses me, sir."

"Rehearsals my ass," O'Sullivan murmurs. "You have something for me, son?" He rustles the permission slips in his hand.

"Sir, yes, sir." Zack pulls his slip out of a green bound book—*Robin Hood, A Play by Don Nigro*, Dawn reads—and hands it to his teacher.

"Perhaps I should have given you two? One for the girlfriend to sign?"

"Sir, don't worry about me and the GF. She knows how important this weekend is and that I'm a team player looking forward to whatever Mother Nature throws my way, sir." Zack winks at Abigail. "Sir, they say that when it gets real cold out there your best chance of survival is spooning, sir."

The class roars.

*What's spooning?* Dawn wonders, and rests her chin in her hands.

"Evans?"

Dawn looks up at her teacher standing over her.

Some of the students begin to moan like zombies.

O'Sullivan's scowl hushes them almost instantly. Dawn curtains her face with one hand. She holds out her slip with the other. The teacher takes it with a gentle hand, turns on his heels, and goes to Elie. He stands over him, waiting.

\*\*\*

"Sir?" Elie asks—wondering, *What does he want?*

"Your slip?"

"Sir, I already gave it in, sir."

O'Sullivan goes through the list in his hand. "Then why don't I have it?"

"Sir, I handed mine in last month, the day after you gave us the form," Elie says, politely. "You told me to leave it on your desk, sir."

"Well I never got it."

*That's impossible,* Elie thinks, looking over at O'Sullivan's desk and catching J.J. and Lance locked in on him, bumping fists. "Sir, maybe—"

"Sir, maybe Osama here decided to chicken out, sir," Lance throws in.

44

"What you talking about, Willis?" Jonathan interjects. "Ahmed isn't afraid of anything." He bows in prayer. "He's got Allah on his side."

"Shut up!" Elie says.

Jonathan turns to Lance, "Maybe Omar's just got something better to do, like pray or 9-11 our asses again?"

"You're such an idiot, you know that?" Elie tells him. "I think you've been sacked one too many times."

"What do you know about football, Al-Qaida?" Jonathan says. "In your country, instead of strapping on shoulder pads to play ball you strap on bombs to kill all."

"I know that QB stands for quarterback, but in your case it means queer boy," Elie retorts.

The class "oohs!"

Jonathan jumps out of his seat. "You shut your a-hole, A-rab."

Elie stands, and blows Jonathan a kiss. "You like it when they pile up on you, don't you, QB?"

Jonathan marches up to Elie. "You shut your sand trap, Habibi."

Elie leans in, "Yeah, or what are you going to do about it?" The class turns deathly silent. He waits for Jonathan's next move.

"Go back to your country." Jonathan reaches for Elie's eyebrow—

O'Sullivan takes a step forward, but stops when Elie grabs Jonathan's wrist.

"This *is* my country, QB." Elie pushes Jonathan's wrist away. "And my name isn't Ahmed or Omar or Al-Qaida. My name is Elie El-Hage. A proud American, born and raised in this country, and I would gladly give my life to protect it ... just like my grandfather did, and my father is doing right now."

"Oh, yeah?" Jonathan turns and struts to his desk, "On whose side, Mohammed?"

The class cheers Jonathan as he raises his arms in victory.

Jeffrey's half smirk is quickly downturned when Jonathan kicks his ankle.

*Fucking bully*, Elie thinks, *one of these days ...* he sucks his teeth and sits.

"You're so awesome," Alex whispers to him, her brown eyes scintillating.

"Are we all done here?" the teacher asks.

"Sir, I believe my permission slip was taken from your desk, sir," Elie says.

O'Sullivan glances over at Jonathan then back at Elie. "Sorry, son. Whatever the reason, school rules: no slip, no trip."

"Sir, but it'll bring down my mark, sir."

O'Sullivan raises his eyebrows and marches to his desk.

*Fucking assholes,* Elie clenches and unclenches his fists.

"All right—" the teacher hobbles back with a blank permission slip "—you've got 'til sixteen-thirty, son." He sets the paper on Elie's desk. "Don't let me down."

"Sir, thank-you, sir." Elie shoots Lance and Jonathan a look. *Nice try assholes.*

Jonathan and Lance seethe their disappointment.

O'Sullivan scans the classroom, then his list. "Okay then, the rest of you I have."

***

Jeffrey and Doris exchange a surprised sigh. Their teacher stops beside them. "Oh, and in case you two think you got out of this one, I want you to know that I personally went to see your mother, Mitchell, and your father, Dalton, and got them to sign the permission slips myself."

*What …?* Jeffrey is momentarily speechless. "Sir, he's not my father, sir."

"No, he's just banging your momma," Ronald cuts in, inciting a stream of giggles.

Jeffrey eyeballs them. "Sir, he's my stepfather and he has no right, sir."

"I can't believe my mom signed that stupid form!" Doris blurts out. "Well, I'm not going!"

"Neither am I," Jeffrey says, as calmly as he can manage. *No need to give these assholes more fuel for their fire.*

"If you miss this weekend," O'Sullivan tells them, "you fail the course. Do you understand?"

They both shrug. *Big fucking deal,* Jeffrey thinks.

The teacher leans in, his hands on each of their backs. His blue eyes soften. "Come on, it's not a punishment, it's going to be fun. I promise you, after this weekend you're going to be begging me to take you out there again."

*Like fuck I will.* Jeffrey sees that Doris is also shaking her head.

O'Sullivan screws up his face. His eyes turn an icy gray. He squeezes the base of their necks. "You make sure you're on that goddamn bus!"

Jeffrey swallows hard and glances at Doris, open-mouthed and frozen in her chair. The entire class seems frozen in their chairs, too, he notes.

O'Sullivan glides across to the blackboard and points at it. "By now," he continues in a chipper tone, "the eight simple rules for survival had better

48

be ingrained in your heads because come tomorrow you will need them more than you'll need your mommies, daddies or even your GFs," he points at Zack, "because, like Schwartz said, you never know what Mother Nature may throw your way."

"Sir, was I right about spooning, sir?" Zack grins.

Nervous laughter flutters. Dawn cocks her head and frowns.

"Sir, why can't I bring food?" Sharon says. "I'm a vegan. I can't eat meat or fish, sir."

"You can eat plants and berries," the teacher responds.

"Sir, I'm going to starve to death, sir," she whines.

"No, you're going to learn to survive," he affirms. "Just make sure you bring everything on your list," he tells the rapt class. "Especially your sleeping bags, unless you want Schwartz spooning with you."

"Sir, can we bring guns?" Jonathan asks over the chuckles. "Let off a few rounds? Do a little target shooting, sir?"

"Are guns on the list, son? No. Your survival kit and knife. That's all."

"Sir, but aren't there wild animals out there, sir?" Rosa stammers.

"Many."

"Sir, cougars and bears, sir?" Heather exclaims.

"Sir," George cuts in, "will we be engaging in any kind of war games, sir?"

"Sir, what about hostiles, like crazy hillbillies?" Zack begins to quote *Deliverance*: "'He got a real purty mouth, ain't he? I bet he can squeal like a'—" Zack squeals like a pig. Some of the boys squeal along with him.

O'Sullivan waves his arms and raises his voice to be heard over the barrage. "No war games, no hostiles, no hillbillies, no pigs. You only need to fear one enemy out there."

\*\*\*

The teacher lets them chew on that for a long moment. The teens shoot accusatory glances across the room, many of which stop on Elie. *Yeah, right, me,* Elie thinks angrily.

"Who? What enemy?" Lance demands.

"Yourself," O'Sullivan says.

*Ourselves …?* Elie is surprised.

"*You* are your worst enemy," O'Sullivan continues. "But by following the eight simple rules for survival you will overcome that. And if by

50

chance you do come face to face with the enemy, you'll know what to do."

"Sir, is that what saved you, sir?" Billy Bob asks.

"Yes, son."

Sharon sits up in her seat and asks, "Sir, were you afraid, sir?"

"Of course, I was." He points at the letter V on the blackboard. "But I vanquished it."

"Sir, how did you get caught, sir?" Billy Bob asks.

"Sir, what happened, sir?" George follows with another question.

Jonathan shifts his head from Billy Bob to George. *Is Johnson getting nervous?* Elie wonders, amused. He quickly chimes in, "Sir, yeah, what happened, sir?"

He motions to Alex and she follows suit, "Sir, please, tell us, sir."

"Tell us, tell us!" Elie pleads, and starts tapping his desk.

Others join in, rattling the classroom. "Tell us, tell us, tell us!"

Jonathan sinks into his chair, Elie notes, and wonders if he's the only one to catch it.

O'Sullivan eyes the clock above the door and holds up his hands. "Alright, alright you bunch of misfits. Settle down!" The class grows silent. "A little American history," he pulls open his desk drawer, "with how I used my wits to take out one of the fifty-four cards." He pulls out a deck of cards, spreads them like a fan, and closes them.

The class oohs.

*Yeah, the fifty-four cards ...* Elie remembers learning about the fifty-four cards on line. How the U.S. military developed them to help their troops identify the most-wanted members of President Saddam Hussein's regime. *Hmm ... I wonder which one The Sarge killed.*

The teacher leans against the front of his desk. "Spring 2003, two days after the toppling of Saddam Hussein's statue. We were flying over Tikrit in search of—"

Proud to have gotten The Sarge to tell his story, Elie turns his attention back to Jonathan—who now grips the corners of his desk as if he'd like to rip the top right off as he eyeballs Jeffrey. *What's up with QB?* Elie wonders.

"... not more than thirteen years old," O'Sullivan continues. "We were sure they were friendlies and began to descend. Just then, they pulled their weapons out from under the sand and opened fire." He aims the deck of cards at the students—"Rat-a-tat-tat!"—and mimes firing a machine gun. The kids jump in their seats. O'Sullivan continues, "It was kill or be killed—"

"Sir, but they were only kids, sir," Sharon says meekly.

"They were soldiers, Jenkins. Damn good soldiers. Real patriots with more balls than most kids today."

Elie notices Jeffrey digging into his sketchpad; tearing the pages with the point of his pencil. *Whoa, him too?*

"Sir, you did what you had to do, sir," George affirms.

"You're damned right, I did. I lost some good men that day."

Elie darts his eyes around the room: Jonathan is intensely locked in on Jeffrey; Jeffrey is insanely fixed on O'Sullivan—the sound of Jeffrey's pencil's erratic scribbling fills the teacher's pauses.

"Damned good men," O'Sullivan says gravely.

Jeffrey suddenly blurts out, "You should have died instead, you bastard."

Elie watches all eyes land on Jeffrey. *Damn, the boy finally grew a pair!*

"Dalton? You say something?" O'Sullivan asks.

Jeffrey's shoulders rise, and his eyelids drop to a squint. *If looks could kill,* Elie thinks. *What bug bit him?*

"See me after school, son."

The class oohs. *They're good at oohing,* Elie muses. *They're missing all the action.* He glances at Jeffrey, then at Jonathan. *I gotta know!* "Sir, what happened then, sir?" he asks.

Jonathan looks daggers at him. Elie smirks, *I don't know what's got you, but I like it.* He stares his enemy square in the eyes.

O'Sullivan spreads his broad hands on either side of his desk and cranes his neck. "I ran out of ammo, son. And I wasn't about to let them take me alive. So I made a run for it. Tried to get back in the chopper when, out of nowhere, out came the big guns. Number forty-seven," he flashes the six of spades, "picked me off and …" The teacher rubs his wounded leg. Again, Elie pans the room. Most of the class sits on the edge of their seat, openmouthed. O'Sullivan licks his meaty lips, obviously savoring the moment, and continues.

\*\*\*

The students pour out of the classroom to the end of first period bell.

"Fucking, Rambo!" Billy Bob says, clicking his heels together. The wheels in his runners jut out. "I didn't know The Sarge was such a war hero." He spins around Scott and George.

"I would've done the same," Scott says.

"You would have shit yourself, Gringo," George needles.

"Fuck you!" Scott pushes him. "I can stand pain."

"Tell me about it." George points at Cindy, and pushes Scott back.

Scott is about to push him back but begins to laugh, "You got me there, *amigo*."

All three boys laugh. Then take a pause.

"I'll bet they did a lot more to him than what he's saying, those fucking A-rabs," Scott says with a sneer.

"Yeah …," Billy Bob and George murmur.

"But The Sarge held on," Billy Bob continues. "With a bullet in his leg and them torturing him and with no hope of a rescue team, he sat there and took it, waited and planned for the right moment."

"Then, bam! Bam! Bam!" Scott cuts in, "he smoked the camelfuckers!"

"Crawled back in the Apache and flew back to base," Billy Bob finishes, gleaming.

"I like the part about how he picked up all his dead men and their body parts and put them in the copter," George says, his brown eyes bright.

"Yeah!" Billy Bob agrees, "And how he tied up card number forty-seven to the landing skid and flew him over Tikrit so they could all see that there is no escape from the strong arm of the—"

"U S OF A!" the three boys holler, "HOO-AH!"

\*\*\*

Alex and Elie roll their eyes at the scene as they approach their lockers hand in hand to get their books for next period. Elie notices Jonathan step out of O'Sullivan's classroom, obviously fuming. "If you ask me," he tells Alex loudly, "I think they *all* fucked up. To be taken out by a bunch of thirteen year-olds …?"

Jonathan charges over and punches Elie's locker door. It smashes shut with a loud bang; Elie doesn't even flinch.

Jonathan storms away.

"What's wrong with him?" Elie mocks aloud. "What's he so pissed about?"

Scott stops in front of Elie. "His father was one of the men who died on that mission, asshole."

"Oh," Elie says.

"And so was his," Scott points at Jeffrey and continues down the hall, followed by Billy Bob and George.

"How was I supposed to know …?" Elie tells Alex. He turns to Jeffrey and mouths a meaningful, "Sorry."

Jeffrey shrugs, closes his locker door and shuffles off.

\*\*\*

Scott and the boys round the corner on the way to English class.

"What?" Billy Bob says, skating backwards, facing Scott. "You're telling me that J.J. and the geek were best friends?"

"Up to the day they brought J.J.'s dad home in a body bag," Scott replies.

"I don't get it," George says, scratching his head. "How's that the geek's fault?"

"It was Dalton's dad who convinced J.J.'s to go on that mission," Scott explains.

George cracks his thick neck and mutters, "Shit, that's pretty fucked up."

"I never knew that," Billy Bob says, stopping on his heels. "No kidding he hates him."

Scott raises his eyebrows. His steel eyes reflect a cold indifference. "At least he knows what happened to his dad … mine's still MIA."

Chapter 4

# RUNNING THE CLOCK

The sound of the final bell rattles the unusually warm and tranquil autumn afternoon. Hooper High's double doors burst open, and students stream into the Indian summer day.

Jackets around their waists, Elie and Alex rush through the school's busy parking lot and jump on Elie's dirt bike. He tries to kick-start it once, twice. On the third attempt, he notices a vacant spot where his spark plug is supposed to be. He wipes the sweat off his brow. "Fuckers!" he vents. "Wait here," he tells Alex, and bolts back into the school. He finds Lance, Scott and Billy Bob in the hallway, smirking. "Alright, guys," Elie says, "give it back."

Lance steps forward. All two hundred and forty-five pounds of him. "What you talking about, cuz," he asks, almost grazing Elie's nose, "give *what* back?"

"My spark plug … please," Elie says firmly.

"Even with a cherry on top, my sand brother," Lance replies, "We don't have nothing that belongs to you. You know."

The three boys hold out their hands—Lance's fingers are smeared with grease.

"Come on," Elie almost begs.

Jonathan comes up behind Elie. "They said they don't have it. Now fuck off!"

"Look, man," Elie says apologetically, "I know you're pissed about this morning, but I swear I didn't know that your father—"

Jonathan sticks his pointy chin out at him. "I said, fuck off!" he barks.

The boys circle Elie, doing their best to intimidate him. He pushes past Billy Bob and tears down the hall.

"That's right, go cry to the teacher," Billy Bob shouts.

"Pussy!" Scott yells.

Elie stops, takes a deep breath and knocks on O'Sullivan's door. The door opens after a moment and Elie sees Jeffrey at his desk, drawing in his sketchpad.

O'Sullivan takes a step forward, towering over the teen, eyebrows raised, "You still here?"

"Sir, something happened to my bike, sir."

"Not my problem, son. Figure it out for yourself."

"Sir, I don't think I'll be able to make it back in time, sir"

"You've got one hour." And with that, the teacher shuts the door.

*** 

Dawn settles among the crisp fallen leaves under the impressive oak tree by the school's front entrance: her favorite place. She finds an acorn by her feet, lifts it to her nose, and inhales its woodsy aroma before tossing it to a plump squirrel collecting her winter stash. She notices the flock of geese flying overhead in V formation, and turns down her music player's volume to hear their honks.

Bang! The school door pops open. She starts and cranks up the volume. An angry looking Elie storms—to the beat—down the cement stairs. The teenage dramas that unfold at the end of the day are like music videos, she decides. *My MTV*.

Elie passes George and Rosa, perched on a step. Dawn stays fixed on the Latino couple, who are making out. The music in her ears slows and George's fingers seem to dance to the rhythm over Rosa's black, voluminous curls. He leans into her and sets his mouth on her fuchsia-glossed lips. *Mmm,* Dawn sighs. The beat picks up again.

She shifts her attention and finds the gorgeous Zack flashing his dazzling smile, arms wrapped around Abigail and Kimberly. *Ahh! They're so lucky,* Dawn thinks, envious, as the trio disappears around the corner.

And—as if switching the channel—she flicks her attention to the parking lot.

***

Scott sits in his red convertible, amused, watching Elie push his bike along. Alex jogs next to him toting both of their knapsacks. *What a fox,* Scott thinks. Elie and Alex pass Billy Bob, who's doing three-sixties with his roller shoes. "Hey, Moskovskaya!" Scott calls out to Alex. "Why don't you trade in your camel jockey and hit up with a mustang ... feel some *real* horsepower." He squeezes the steering wheel, and fantasizes running his hands up her long, slender legs. He grabs himself.

Ronald neighs in the back seat.

Cindy jumps into the front passenger side and punches Scott's arm. "I heard that!"

"Hey, I'm just breaking their balls," Scott says, loudly.

Heather smacks Scott's headrest. "What are we waiting for?"

"Him," Scott says, raising his square jaw at Jonathan sitting alone in his blue Ford pick-up parked next to them. *Get over it, dude,* Scott thinks, noticing Jonathan's nostrils flaring, eyes fixed on the school. "And him." Scott points at Lance who takes a paper bag out from under the pick-up's bed cover.

Lance opens the Ford's passenger door to get in as Jonathan slams his shut and heads back to the school. Lance throws Billy Bob a look. "The fuck's up with him?"

Billy Bob skates toward Jonathan. "Where you going, J?"

Jonathan barrels forward.

Sharon chases after him. "Baby, what's wrong?"

Scott snorts as he watches Jonathan flick his hand at Sharon like he were shooing a fly. *You've been dicked, baby, move on!* he thinks, trying to hold back his laugher.

Cheeks flushed, Sharon hurries off, almost bumping into Dawn who ambles away, brushing the leaves off her black tube skirt.

Scott chuckles and the rest in the car begin to snigger.

Lance leans an elbow on the convertible's driver's side door and juts his chin out at Billy Bob—all the while glaring at the gang in the vehicle. They all give the slightest of nods and keep their laughter to themselves.

Let me catch a ride with you guys?" Lance asks Scott.

"Hop in," Scott answers, then cranes his neck over his windshield and calls out, "Hey, Swifty, you coming?"

"Uhh … No … I'll catch you guys later," Billy Bob answers, eyes on his sister. "I got to go pack." And he wheels off toward Sharon.

Lance plops in between Ronald and Heather, "Let's roll."

Ronald pulls a stack of posters out from his knapsack and holds it up: VOTE CHARLES M. COLLINS FOR MAYOR printed in blue under a handsome photo of his father. "I promised my dad I'd get at least fifty of these up before I went home."

"Then fifty it'll be, my man!" Lance says, giving him fist props.

Scott looks at Lance through the rearview. "You packed for tomorrow, bro?"

"Not only for tomorrow, my brother. I'm packed for tonight. Six packed." Lance tears open the paper bag he fished out of the Ford and flashes beer cans. "You know."

***

Jeffrey switches from 3B to 5B pencils; skillfully building up his sketch's shading details. There's a knock at the door as he glides a fingertip over a strong line. He eyes the wall clock over the classroom door—3:45—and turns to O'Sullivan, who knits his brow and pushes himself out of his wooden chair. The teacher opens the door, taking a breath as if readying to speak, and says nothing. Looking past O'Sullivan's ear, Jeffrey sees Jonathan. His grey eyes seem ferocious and ... *desperate*, Jeffrey thinks. The teacher takes a step forward, closing the door quietly behind him. Wiping his lead-stained fingertip on his thigh, Jeffrey strains to hear Jonathan and O'Sullivan in the hallway. Impulsively, he creeps to the door and, after pressing his ear to it for a long moment, he opens it a crack.

O'Sullivan pulls Jonathan into the classroom directly across and shuts the door. Through the door's smoked window, Jeffrey can make out Jonathan burying his head into O'Sullivan's chest. After a moment, the teacher puts his arms around him and both move out of view.

*What the ...?* Jeffrey goes back to his seat, confused. He grabs his 5B but can't focus on his drawing. The lines and details blur. He looks up at the clock.

\*\*\*

Elie pulls into his double driveway. Motor still running, he kicks down the bike stand, jumps off, and sprints up the cedar green-paneled bungalow's trim front yard—automatically nodding at the American flag waving high over the entrance. He wipes his greasy fingers on his pant leg, and opens the door. A bouquet of mint, ginger, cloves, and cinnamon wafts into his nostrils as rhythmic Arabic music sails out the opened door and into the street. He checks his watch. 4:25. *"Teta!"* he calls out to his grandmother. "I've got something I need you to sign."

\*\*\*

When the classroom door finally opens, Jeffrey is shaken out of his daze. The wall clock reads 4:26. O'Sullivan approaches. Jeffrey flips his sketchpad closed, then slides both pencils into its spiral coil. He holds the pad against his chest like a shield; he's ready for dismissal. O'Sullivan's silent beside him. *Weird.* Jeffrey reaches for his knapsack, but the teacher puts a firm hand on his chest and tenderly pushes him back into his seat.

"So? You wish it was me instead." O'Sullivan lets out a heavy sigh and begins to pace around him. "Me too, son. Me too … I wish I was killed instead of your father, instead of Johnson's father, instead of everybody else's father that I lost that day. But the truth is—" he stops and looks Jeffrey square in the eye "—there's nothing anybody could have done to change what happened." He points at Jeffrey. "But you blame me, just like Johnson blames you." He gazes deep into Jeffrey's hazel eyes, "You think that's right?"

Jeffrey doesn't know what to say.

O'Sullivan sits on the desk and rubs his damaged thigh. "I need you to be there this weekend, son." He squeezes Jeffrey's arm. "Your father was a great soldier. Best of the best. And you … you have it inside you … I know. Let me show you," he pleads, "it's the least I can do. Okay?"

Pushing his glasses up, Jeffrey offers a hesitant nod and a half smile—*just let me the hell out of here!*

66

"I promise, after this weekend, you'll feel like a new man." O'Sullivan gives Jeffrey an affectionate slap on the back. "Now go home and pack. I'll see you at o-six-hundred hours, son."

Chapter 5

# YOU WOULDN'T WANT TO BE IN MY KICKS

Jeffrey barely notices the splendid pinks, oranges, blues and grays of the late-afternoon sky as he hurries along the tree-lined suburban street. The air is warm, but he is shivering, and peeking over his shoulder—even more than usual. A strong breeze sneaks a swirl of dried leaves up behind him. He whips around and scans the rows of well-kept bungalows—meant mostly for military families who cannot find adequate housing at the nearby base. Each home waves the same red, white, and blue. Colored panels, bay windows, reflecting flat screens, trim lawns and hedges. Each a carbon-copy of the last. The streets are empty. And it's a long way home. *One block at a time*, he reminds himself. With his eyes now to the ground, he continues on, careful to avoid the clumps of dead leaves—his ears need to keep alert. He peeks ahead. *Almost at the curb!* he tells himself, and picks up his pace. *What's that?* He's startled by a noise from the hedges. The gathering dusk doesn't allow for much clarity … he backs away, trying to see through the evergreen shrubs. Another noise! His heel slips off the unanticipated curb. A black sedan suddenly comes to a stop behind him. He turns.

O'Sullivan leans over the passenger seat and smiles. "Need a lift?"

Jeffrey shakes his head.

"Come on, hop in, son. It'll give you more time to pack."

"Sir, I'm enjoying the walk, sir." *No fucking way I'm getting in a car with you.*

"Suit yourself." O'Sullivan smiles and drives off.

Jeffrey waits until his teacher's car is halfway down the street before crossing. He puts one foot in front of the other when tires suddenly screech, an engine roars, and a deafening hum fills his ears as a vehicle speeds toward him. He's caught in the headlights. It's coming straight for him! But the tires slide to a stop. He stumbles backwards onto the sidewalk.

"Hey, geek!" Cindy shouts. Heather stands on the back seat of Scott's convertible and moons Jeffrey.

Scott reaches behind and grabs Lance's beer.

"Hey!" Lance protests.

Scott whips the can. It bashes Jeffrey's forehead and knocks him down.

"That'll teach you for checking out my girl's ass, creep!" Ronald hollers as the car peels off.

Jeffrey wipes the oozing blood off his forehead with a beer-soaked sleeve and feels the ground for his glasses. He finds them and a blue Ford pick-up parked across the street behind a large van comes into focus. *Shit. Not him, too.* He whirls and slams into Jonathan, who has stepped out from behind the hedge.

Before Jeffrey can realize what's happening, Jonathan has knocked him down, dragged him through the thorny bushes, and pinned him face down on the ground. Jeffrey can hardly move—he's lying on one arm, the other's being twisted behind him.

Jonathan presses his strong slender body down with what feels like two hundred pounds of muscle. "So what are you, buddy buddy with the A-Rab now? Allies with the enemy? What, d'you forget who killed our dads? Huh?" He pushes Jeffrey's face into the damp ground.

"I guess you did because you thought that was real funny in class, didn't you? Well, let's see how funny you think it is this weekend when we have your skeez on her knees giving her what you can't. And she'll enjoy it. Dora the Whora ... She'll be begging my boys to run a train through her. You saw the way she checked out Scott? I bet she can't wait for it."

"Fuck off!" Jeffrey struggles, but Jonathan has him pinned tight.

"You like it, don't you, geek? Maybe you want us to run a train through you instead?" Jonathan pushes into him, hard.

Jeffrey squirms, trying to free himself. "Fucking ... kill you!"

"You'll what?" Jonathan laughs. "You don't have the balls, freak."

The distinct sound of a motorbike approaches. Jonathan jumps to his feet and kicks Jeffrey in the ribs. "But I do." Jonathan points like he's holding a gun at him. "You'd better watch yourself in the woods this weekend. I might mistake you for a rabbit." He pulls the invisible trigger, "Pow," sprints to his truck, and peels off.

Jeffrey pushes through the shrubbery, stumbles onto the street, and lands on the hard pavement.

The motorbike screeches to a halt, stopping inches from Jeffrey's face.

"What the fuck's the matter—" Elie takes in the bleeding forehead and muddy clothes. "Whoa, what the hell happened to you?"

Jeffrey doesn't answer; he brushes the dirt off.

"Those assholes again?"

Jeffrey runs his fingers over his gash and feels his warm blood oozing. "Ah, fuck!"

"You should do something about it." Elie tells him.

Jeffrey uses the hem of his t-shirt to wipe the blood off his forehead. "There's nothing anybody can do anything about."

The boys exchange a sympathetic glance.

"Yeah, I hear you," Elie says. "Fuckers fucked me over too."

"Guess you didn't make it back to school in time with your permission slip, huh?" Jeffrey looks down the road.

Elie shrugs.

"Maybe it's for nothing, but The Sarge went by here a few minutes ago." Jeffrey points in the direction and perceives a hopeful smile on Elie's face that quickly fades.

"Nah," Elie says, "what's the use? The bastard doesn't want me there."

"I wish we could trade, man," Jeffrey says. "Straight up."

"Trust me, you wouldn't want to be in my kicks," Elie grumbles. "Come on, hop on. I'll give you a lift."

"No, I'm okay." Jeffrey bends to pick up his knapsack, favoring his sore shoulder, steadying himself against his throbbing knees, the piercing pain in his ribs, the dull ache in his head. He slides his knapsack up over his left shoulder and scuffs off.

"Hey!" Elie yells as he kick-starts his bike.

Jeffrey turns.

"You and your girlfriend better watch your asses this weekend," Elie yells. "Just sayin'." He gives a meaningful nod and rides off.

"She's not my girlfriend!" Jeffrey shouts over the roar.

Chapter 6

## *I* EMBARRASS *YOU?*

Doris growls. Her entire body convulses. Her face distorts grotesquely. She holds her hands out in front of her and watches outstretched fingers become thicker, longer, hairy, clawed.

"Doris!"

Doris screeches painfully.

"Doris!"

Doris doesn't hear the yelling. She roars.

"DORIS!" her mother screams even louder, turning off the blaring television to end David's

74

transformation scene in *An American Werewolf in London*. "Are you deaf?"

Doris feels she's been smacked out of her imagination. It takes her a moment to realize that her mother is standing in front of her. Cora. The nametag on her nutmeg colored uniform hangs crookedly. Cora—a cheap, older knock-off of herself, Doris thinks. *She makes me sick.* The teen jumps off the beaten couch. "No, are you?"

"How many times have I told you not to put the TV on so loud?" Cora stands, both hands on her hips.

Doris automatically mimics the stance. "How many times have I told *you* I don't want to go on that trip?"

"Hmm? Trip? … Oh, yeah, the trip." Cora returns to the front entrance where she dropped her coat, shopping bag, and a doggie bag from work. "Timmy said it would be good—"

"Timmy, Mom, *Timmy*?" Doris chases after her. "You screwed him, didn't you?"

"Hmm?" Cora picks the greasy bag of leftovers off the floor, "I brought you some dinner, honey."

"I'm talking to you, Mom," she says, tailing her into the kitchen. "Why did you sign that slip?"

Cora sets the small package on the counter. "It's cold but I can warm it up."

Doris points at the phone laying on the bill-cluttered kitchen table. "You call him up right now and tell him I'm not going."

Cora tears open the bag: chicken wings and fries. "Last night's special," she says with a smile. "Still good."

Doris catches a whiff of the day-old barbeque wings—her stomach churns when she notices some of them have been bitten into. "Did the special run from eight p.m. 'til now, Mom?"

"Let me warm these up for you." Cora tosses the wings and fries into a chipped bowl, pops open the microwave and glances at its digital clock. "Shoot! 4:55 already? I'm gonna be late for work."

"What were you serving after three a.m., Mom? Hmm?" *Jesus.* She tries to erase the images that are forming in her head.

"You should see the dress I got today ... absolutely gorgeous." Cora places the bowl in the crusty microwave. "I'll show it to you in a minute."

"I don't want to see the dress, just answer my question." Doris feels an uncomfortable sensation along her spine and neck, like her cells are exploding, one by one, she believes.

Cora considers the buttons on the microwave. "Do you think two minutes will do it?"

Doris stomps her Converse High Tops as though she were two years old again. "I asked you a question."

Cora punches in one minute and rummages through the mostly bare, oil-stained cupboards as she dances, hums and sings a cappella to Joan Jett's "I Love Rock 'n Roll".

"Mom," Doris groans, tugging at her purple-streaked hair. *I must have killed someone in a past life to deserve this pathetic excuse for a mother.*

Cora swings her hips.

"Mom," Doris says through gritted teeth, clasping her left wrist. *Chill ... chill ... chill, girl,* she tells herself, pressing her fingertips into the spikes of her bracelet.

Cora flails her arms while she belts out the chorus.

"Mom!" Doris screams as she spins her mother around. "Why did you sign that fucking slip?"

"Let me get that dress." Cora steps around her daughter and heads for the shopping bag by the front door.

Doris watches the garment slither out. Gold. Sequined. Her mother holds it against her breasts.

It will be low cut on her slim figure. And too short. *Miles* too short. *Slut!*

"Do you think it makes me look pale?" Cora asks, dancing with it.

Doris seizes the dress. "Mother, what do I have to do to get you to listen to me?" The microwave oven beeps, but Doris keeps her mother pinned—with the sheer force of her gaze—to where she stands. "I am not going on that goddamn trip."

Cora takes a step back and looks at her daughter. "You have to, honey," she says softly.

Doris feels she's finally being acknowledged for the first time tonight. "Why?" she pleads.

"You and the Dalton boy … you're in shells. You both need to get out of them and Tim—Sergeant O'Sullivan—guaranteed that after this trip you're going to be new people. That this trip is going to help you. Toughen you up and make you forget about all the bad things that have ever happened to you."

"What bad things, Mom?" She leans right into her mother, "Oh, you mean what your boyfriend did to me?"

"Come on, honey. You know that never happened." Cora's face reddens.

"Right, I made it all up." Doris crosses her arms and presses the barbed bracelets into her ribs.

78

"You know how your imagination runs wild, baby, with all those violent movies you watch. You created all that in your head. I'm talking about your father, hon. Still missing. We don't even know if he's alive." Cora reaches to touch her daughter's hair but Doris shifts her head away. Cora frowns, but continues speaking softly. "I can understand that that would make you hostile. That's why I don't say anything about the way you dress and act and—"

"Embarrassed? *I* embarrass *you?* No. No. *You* embarrass *me.* Coming to my school ... calling me a liar in front of the guidance councilor. Screaming. Now everyone in school thinks I fucked your boyfriend. *That's* why I'm hostile!" Cora holds a hand to her heart and gasps to catch her breath. *I hope you drop dead right here!* Doris, still clutching her mother's dress, turns and heads for the living room, then whips around and goes right at her mother again. "*I* imagine things?" Doris yells, poking her own chest. "You disgust me. I was fuckin' raped and you know it. And I'm not crazy and Daddy isn't missing, nor is he dead. He ran away, Mother! He ran away from *you.*"

Cora steps back. "Ran away? Why ... why would he run away from me?"

"Because you shamed him! You fucked all his army buddies, all his friends. You took a proud man and crushed him. How could he even look at his little girl and not feel worthless?"

Cora winces.

"But I know he'll come for me some day, Mother. Not for you. I need to toughen up?" She sees her mother's eyes well up with pain. "You are the weakest person I've ever seen. Cora the Whora, isn't that what they call you? Why, you'd fuck a dog for a sleazy dress!" Threads snap and gold flecks spatter as Doris tears the dress in half.

Cora's open palm lands with such force that it knocks Doris into the wall. "Oh, no!" The mother cups her hand over her mouth.

*I can't believe she hit me.* "You fucking bitch!" Doris cries, pressing her fingers into her stinging cheek.

Cora falls to her knees and wails, "I'm sorry!"

Doris grabs her knapsack off the hook by the door and thunders out.

"Doris!" Cora cries out. "I'm so sorry!"

Doris stomps down the bungalow's creaky front steps. She manages to hold back her tears until she's a few houses down. Then she comes apart, those cells going haywire all through her body. She pulls out her phone and texts: NEED 2 C

U AQAP (As quickly as possible). CLAB (Crying like a baby). R U HOME YET?

## Chapter 7

## I DON'T WANT IT IN ME!

Jeffrey stands before his front door—about to let himself in—and takes a moment to study himself in the door's glass window. *Shit*, he's surprised by the size of the gash on his forehead. He pulls his hood down, trying to conceal the wound. His cell phone buzzes. Doris's text message. The door swings open.

Sergeant First Class Warren Singleton, fully dressed in his Army best and "brown round" hat, reeking of Chrome cologne, steps out and towers over him. "Where the hell have you been?"

Jeffrey doesn't flinch; he slips his phone back into the front pocket of his knapsack, and walks right by him.

Warren slams the door shut and follows behind. He reaches and seizes Jeffrey's hoodie, stopping him in the middle of the living room. "I'm talking to you, boy. Don't you walk away." He yanks Jeffrey's hood off. Jeffrey stands with his back to his stepfather. "Look at you, you look like a girl." He tugs at Jeffrey's shaggy, shoulder-length hair. "Look at me when I talk to you, boy." Warren spins him around and the man's eyes widen. "What the hell happened to your head? Let me see that." He leans in. The teen takes a step back. "I said let me—" Warren takes a step closer. His nostrils flare. "Have you been drinking, son?"

Not wanting to meet his gaze, Jeffrey stares at the one-inch scar over Warren's left eye—*so dark against the brown skin* ... "Sir, you're not my father, sir."

The man pushes Jeffrey's hair back and glowers at the gash and the scratches on his face. "Who did this?"

"Sir, it doesn't matter, sir."

"Why do you stink of beer?"

Jeffrey raises his eyes to him and struggles to swallow his anguish. "Sir, it's all part of the course outline. A beer can across the head, bloodstains"— he flashes his bloody sleeve—"and living in constant horror are what you and my mom subjected me to when you forced me into that program. It's bad enough I didn't want to go to that school in the first place ... now you're forcing me to go on that stupid trip? Those bastards are going to do everything they can to make this weekend a living hell for me, sir."

Warren visibly swallows. Jeffrey watches the walnut-sized Adam's apple rise and fall. "I put you in that program to toughen you up, son. You have to learn to muscle back." The man circles Jeffrey as he speaks. "Your father was one of the boldest and toughest soldiers I ever had the privilege of serving with, and I know that you have it in you, too." Warren stops in front of the boy. "Trust me, if you push back, they will back away."

"Sir, maybe I don't have it in me." *I don't want it in me!* he wants to say. "I can't be a soldier. I don't believe in violence—that's what got my father killed. Sir, please, call Sergeant O'Sullivan and tell him I won't be making the trip, sir." Jeffrey stares at the gold metal badge centered on Warren's campaign hat. *This We'll Protect,* he reads. *Yeah, right.*

"I'm sorry, son," Warren says gravely, "that's not an option."

"Sir … I don't trust him, sir." *Or your fucking hat.*

"O'Sullivan's a decorated hero, son!" Warren slaps the medals on his chest.

"Sir, please don't make me go, sir," Jeffrey pleads. *I'd like to rip that "brown round" off your head. See the look on your face when I stomp it flat.*

"There's a backpack in your room. Everything on the list is on your bed." He pokes Jeffrey's chest. "I suggest you go and pack."

Jeffrey looks into his eyes, "If my father was alive …," he mutters. *He'd shit in your hat,* he almost says aloud.

Warren leans into him. "If your father was alive he'd be ashamed of you. There's no way I'm going to let his son grow up to be a coward. I have too much respect for him."

"Is that why you married his wife?" Jeffrey spurts.

Before Warren can respond, Olivia glides into the living room wearing her blue evening gown. *She's so beautiful,* Jeffrey thinks. *Elegant. Even with the rollers in her hair.*

"Honey, I'm almost ready— Jeffrey!" she stops and smiles at her son.

Jeffrey bows his head. *Don't worry her*, he thinks.

Olivia floats over, takes his chin in her hand, and leans in to kiss his cheek. "Oh, my goodness!" she cups her mouth, glances at Warren, then back at her son. "Honey, what happened?"

Jeffrey searches her kind hazel eyes. *Mommy!* He wants to cry. *Help me!* But instead, he gives her a half-smile and shrugs.

"Who did this to you?" Olivia examines the gash. "Warren, we should call the police."

"He's all right, Liv." Warren says, evenly.

"It's only a cut, Mom," Jeffrey tells her.

"Let me get something for that." Olivia starts for the stairs.

"I said he's all right," Warren repeats firmly, stopping her in her tracks. "Jeffrey was on his way up to pack."

"Pack! Oh, I'm so glad, hon." She turns to her husband. "See, Warren? I told you he'd change his mind." She proceeds to the kitchen, "Come, let me warm up your supper," she tells her son.

Jeffrey sets his knapsack down and follows her.

"We're going to be late," Warren points out impatiently.

Olivia touches the rollers in her hair. "Oh!" Her eyes flit from husband to son.

"It's all right, Mom." *You'd better do what he says*, Jeffrey thinks. "I'm not hungry now. I'll have it later."

"The steak's in the blue Tupperware," Olivia patters, "The salad—"

"Olivia!" Warren snaps.

"Be ready in ten." She flutters away.

Jeffrey picks up his knapsack and lumbers off.

"Oh, and one more thing, son," Warren tells him, sternly.

Jeffrey stops at the bottom step, his back to Warren again.

"If for any reason you miss that bus tomorrow, you'll get your wish and no longer be at that school. Come Monday morning you'll be in boot camp, with me. And if you think *they're* giving you a hard time …."

A heavy silence weighs on Jeffrey.

*** 

Warren turns to the television. It's on mute. A few dozen turkeys peck the ground while a smiling farmer scatters seeds. *Where the hell did I put it?* He finds the television remote and settles in his tan

87

leather La-Z-Boy armchair as Jeffrey trudges up the stairs. Warren turns up the volume on *HTV's Live at Five*. The turkeys gobble in disharmony yet almost appear to be smiling, too, he thinks with a smirk.

"Now that's talking turkey," the anchorwoman says.

Warren laughs.

"And they'll be arriving at your local supermarket just in time for the Thanksgiving holiday. Now in other news, it got pretty wild at Club Rave On last night in downtown Hope, and I mean wild. The following story is graphic and intended for *mature* viewers … Fifteen arrests were made when police were called to break up a brawl."

Warren shakes his head at the footage of police officers securing the scene with yellow tape.

"Apparently, a male and female in their late teens began having sexual intercourse on the dance floor. Other patrons soon joined in and security rushed to intervene. It is claimed the two youths became quite aggressive when all were asked to leave, so bouncers tried to physically remove the couple from the premises. The two average-sized youths overpowered the burly bouncers. When other patrons tried to help calm the situation, chaos ensued, a brawl broke out and the club went from sex to violence."

Warren lifts his eyes to the ruckus coming from Jeffrey's room above. He smiles, pleased with himself, and turns his attention back to the news report: shards of broken glass on the pavement—what's left of the nightclub's front door.

"Police were on the scene moments later in riot squad gear. Despite the use of pepper spray and batons, some patrons were extremely difficult to restrain. Taser guns were then employed. However, the teens who allegedly instigated the chaos could not be restrained. These two were not affected by the Taser darts and managed to scratch and bite their way out of the club. The bouncers sustained serious wounds and one officer's face was severely lacerated; officers are still combing the area in search of his ear. Police warn the community to take great caution. The two assailants are extremely dangerous."

A close-up on a bloody handprint zooms out; it's on the hood of a police car. The camera follows a blood trail that leads to—and stops at—a blood-stained nine-foot high cedar picket fence that separates the neighboring building.

"They fled the scene at what witnesses describe as "super-human" speed, jumping and leaping over cars and fences. If seen, police insist you do not approach them. Call your local authorities immediately."

"Goddamned kids today," Warren grumbles, and switches the station.

*** 

An hour later, Jeffrey sits on his bed. His room is in shambles. He grabs a camouflage field jacket that has landed on his television screen and is about to hurl it again when he notices the nametags:

DALTON on the right, U.S. ARMY on the left. He slumps down on his bed. *Dad*. He runs his fingers over the name, hugs the coat and cries.

Outside his window, the roar of an engine disturbs the quiet neighborhood. Jeffrey checks the street and sees Elie zoom by on his motorbike.

## Chapter 8

# GOD, SHE'S AWESOME

Elie pulls up to a house much like his own—except for the red panels—and parks his motorbike next to a green Buick Century facing out in the driveway. The double garage door is open, and Alex—dressed in a crisp black martial arts uniform secured with a green belt—kicks and punches a bag in unison to an instructional video playing on her laptop. The computer flashes from its roost: a red metal tool cabinet. Elie enters dragging his feet and plops into the threadbare loveseat by the door that leads into the house.

Alex pounds the bag with precision and skill—her auburn ponytail snaps from side to side with every hit. "So?" she says, wiping the sweat above her lip.

Elie flings the permission slip in the air. "He was gone by the time I got there."

"And?" she asks, side kicking the bag in the area of a human groin.

*Ow!* he thinks. He raises his thick brows. "What?"

"What—HI-YA!— are you going to do about it?"

Elie shakes his head. "There's nothing anybody can do anything about."

"Bullshit!" She kicks the bag hard.

"I'm not going," he says, flatly.

"You don't go, I don't go." She jabs the bag at the heart this time, he notes.

"That's not fair," he tells her.

She kicks the top of the bag. *Nice! Definite brain injury*, he thinks.

"Then go see him," she says.

"The Sarge?" Elie sits up. "At his home?"

"Duh!"

93

"Are you kidding?" He flops back into the cushion. Dust poofs out in small clouds on either side of him.

"What are you, afraid of him?" she asks, and grabs the bag, steadying it, as she stares at him.

"No." He stands up and puffs out his chest. "I'm not afraid of anything."

"Then go!" she yells, and thrusts the bag toward him.

Elie swiftly grips the bag, and, without dropping his eyes from hers, lets go of it and snatches the permission slip off the ground. "I don't even know where he lives."

Alex jab jabs with her right, throws a left hook and roundhouses the bag. She pulls off her gloves, grabs a towel from a hook, wipes the sweat off her face and neck, and clicks off the video—the screen's background photo is a black and white of her grandparents both wearing *ushankas*—trapper hats—and posing in front of the Kremlin.

She "411"s *Tim O'Sullivan* and goes down a long list of addresses. "Tim, Tim, Timothy O'Sullivan … only one in Hooper! 116 King Street. Give me your phone," she orders.

Elie complies.

She turns on his GPS, punches in the coordinates and hands the phone back to him. "Now move your ass, soldier!"

Elie beams. *God, she's awesome*. He leans in for a kiss.

"There's no time for that," she giggles, and pushes him playfully. He pushes her back and they begin to spar. "Will you stop?" she laughs. "Go!"

Elie starts to head out, glances at her laptop, and turns back to her. "Do me a favor," he says, "Google the fifty-four cards. Card number forty-seven."

"Why? What's up?" she asks.

"Just curious." He jumps on his bike and takes off, passing Scott's convertible a few houses down, as they drop off Cindy at her home. Yellow-paneled, Elie notices. *Like the yellow stars on China's flag*, he figures.

Chapter 9

# WHO'S OUT THERE?

The convertible pulls up in front of a blue-paneled bungalow. Ronald jumps out of the car and extends a hand to Heather. "M'lady." She giggles, takes it, and steps out. Ronald pulls her in close, wraps his arms around her slim waist, and presses his lips against hers. Sliding fingers into her soft blond locks, he runs the other hand down the small of her back. The porch lights flick on.

Heather jerks away, "Oh, oh, got to go." She pecks Ronald on the lips, and trots up to her front door.

"Damn …" Ronald murmurs.

Scott, in the driver's seat, shakes his head. "That boy's whipped, bro."

"You know," Lance replies, and takes a swig of beer.

Ronald returns and jumps in the back seat. "What does a brother have to do, man?" he exhales.

"You're almost there, bro," Scott cheers on, winking at Lance.

"It's not easy," Ronald says.

"'Specially with a teasy," Scott needles.

Before Ronald can speak, Lance interjects, "Better get on it, son. Her pop's a Sixty-Eight W. Those MOs get moved around faster than trade bait before an NFL deadline. She'll be bounced before you know it. New town. New clown."

"Who are you calling clown, dawg?" Ronald says, one eyebrow raised. "I'm in stealth mode. I'm a brother undercover. Come this weekend … forget about the sleeping bags. Better bring earplugs if you want to survive. 'Cause I'm going to have my boo howlin' at the moon."

Lance howls. "My man!" he turns and fist bumps Ronald.

O'Sullivan sits at his small dining table, halfway through a frozen dinner. Photos of his glory days with army buddies clutter the gray walls. Five pill bottles labeled WATER PURIFICATION TABLETS sit on the table. One bottle is open, its green pills emptied into a bowl. A fork full of spicy chicken cacciatore hasn't made it to his mouth yet—he holds it mid-air, choking down instead the six o'clock news.

> "Similar incidents have been reported in rave clubs along the East Coast in the last two weeks," the anchorman reports. "Although not confirmed, police suspect they may stem from a new drug on the streets."

"Son of a bitch." He turns off the television and picks up the phone. Punches in three numbers, changes his mind, and slams the phone on the table. There's a knock at his front door. "Who the hell …?" He hobbles over and swings it open.

Elie holds out the signed permission slip as if he were praying. "Sir, please, sir?"

O'Sullivan glares at him. "You've got a lot of balls, son. Coming to my house, banging on my door, disturbing my meal and taking up my valuable time to give me a document you've had over a month to hand in."

"Sir, I—" Elie begins to mutter.

"I like that. No matter what was thrown your way, you never gave up. Now *that's* what I'm talking about. See you at o-six-hundred hours." He takes the slip.

"Sir, thank-you, sir!" Elie salutes him.

O'Sullivan holds back a grin, nods and returns the salute. *There may be hope for that one*, he thinks.

\*\*\*

Under an unlit lamppost, Jonathan sits low in his pick-up truck in the dark, peering over the window at his teacher's gray-paneled bungalow. He watches Elie trot down O'Sullivan's front steps, hop on his bike and ride away. "Fucker!" Jonathan punches the dashboard and drives off.

\*\*\*

Jeffrey has laid the army fatigues neatly on a chair and is stuffing his backpack. *The Howling* plays on his screen—its tattered DVD case rests next to it. He hears Warren's car engine rev and, at the window, watches him back up and brake suddenly—the red convertible with Scott and his gang cruises by the driveway. Jeffrey flattens his back against the wall and cranes to peek out the window. The convertible continues on. *Go*, he tries to compel Warren and his mother to leave, and moments later, when they do, he heaves a long sigh. And follows it with another.

*** 

"Let him by," Ronald murmurs to Scott.

Scott pulls the car over halfway down the block and Lance keeps his hands low as he skillfully rolls a joint.

The boys watch Warren come up alongside and they each offer polite nods as he drives past them.

"Shit, man," Ronald whispers, "don't want to run into him. Mean as a snake, I hear."

"Reminds me of my dad," Lance seals the joint.

"Reminds me of *both* your dads," Scott sneers.

"Fuck you!" Lance and Ronald throw back at him.

Scott snickers and is about to drive off but hesitates, foot still on the brake pedal. He glances the rearview. "Lookie, lookie," he utters, and pops a U-turn.

*** 

Jeffrey remains against the wall, completely engrossed in *The Howling*: Marsha is poised behind a bonfire. She slips off her black leather wrap-around dress. Her splendor bewitches Bill.

A noise outside—*like a garbage can tipped over*—startles Jeffrey. He scans the area and doesn't notice anything out of the ordinary. *Raccoons*, he thinks, and turns back to the film.

The bonfire blazes in the misty forest. Marsha and Bill lie on the earth, mouths and naked bodies pressing into each other. Jeffrey is aroused.

Another noise. He darts his eyes from the window to the television and back again. This movie. He's seen it over a hundred times, and still he's mesmerized when Bill pulls back and reveals his long pointed canines. Marsha squirms beneath him, snarling, electrified by the start of her own transformation.

BANG! Jeffrey jumps back in terror. BANG! he ducks beneath the windowsill. BANG! Trembling, he scans the room for his phone. BANG! BANG! BANG! He forces himself up and sees Doris gawking at him, holding on to the window ledge for dear life.

"You scared the hell out of me!" Jeffrey screams at her through the glass.

On the screen, Bill howls thunderously. Jeffrey watches him become overwhelmed with unbearable pain and absolute ecstasy.

"I texted you!" Doris yells back, though she, too, is captured by the erotic scene.

Eyes glued on *The Howling*, Jeffrey unclasps the lock, lifts open the window, and mumbles, "Sorry, I got drilled and grilled before I got the chance—"

"Fucking bitch! Fucking bitch!" Doris cries as she pulls herself up over the windowsill, eyes on the film.

\*\*\*

The convertible pulls up next to a half bare oak tree and Lance lights up the joint. The boys scope Doris climb in through Jeffrey's window and get full view of her lacy lilac thong again.

"Now that's what I'm talking about," Scott says. "She keeps Britney Spearing me, I'm gonna tap that ass."

"Well, if you like skanky panky," Ronald replies.

"President Obama, my Johnson does not discriminate," Scott takes the joint from Lance.

"Neither does mine, my brother, but I wouldn't touch that with your granddaddy's—" Ronald takes two condoms out of his jacket pocket and flashes them, "—unless I was covered two times."

Scott chokes on his toke from laughter.

"Speaking of Johnsons, what up with J.J.?" Lance asks.

"J.J.'s gonna catch up with us later," Scott wheezes, trying to keep the smoke in his lungs.

Ronald takes the joint from Scott.

"Swifty?" Lance asks.

"Swift is staying in, said he has to modify his hiking boots," Scott answers.

"That boy is one crazy motherfucker if he thinks he's going to roll through them woods on those wheels," Lance says.

"You ask me, they're both crazy, him and his sister." Ronald releases the smoke. "Must be in their genes. See the way Sharon checks J.J.? She's fucking obsessed." He takes another toke. "She don't get it. J.J. Humpty Dumpty'd her ass," he passes the joint to Lance.

"I bet it bothers Swifty," Lance takes a long toke, "I know I'd be pissed if I had a sis and one of you'd be bangin' her." He passes the joint to Scott.

"If he's supposed to feel what she feels, I wonder if he's feeling her pain shame right now," Ronald manages to mumble as he takes the joint from Scott.

"I wonder if he was feeling what she was feeling when my man J.J. was poppin' her," Lance slurs. "You know."

Ronald holds out the roach. The three boys look at one another, bloodshot eyes drooping, mouths half-open, minds a-daze.

Chapter 10

# PISSED

Around the corner from Alex's house, Jonathan seethes in his pick-up, his right hand clasped firmly on a maple wood baseball bat. *I lost some good men that day,* O'Sullivan's words echo in his head, *Damned good men.* Jonathan watches Alex pummel a boxing bag from the open door of her garage.

He remembers being ten, outside of *his* garage with Jeffrey. They both had BMX bikes—Jeffrey's was green and his was blue—and they were trying to pop wheelies. Jeffrey was able to keep his up for a five-second count. *Fucker always beat me by a second*. Jonathan's face relaxes a moment and a grin escapes him. He recalls seeing Jeffrey's dad pull up in an army jeep that afternoon. Watching the man hop out of the vehicle and march toward them. Noticing how the man's camouflage did not help him blend in with the surroundings.

"Hi boys," said Mr. Dalton, patting their heads.

"Hi, Dad," Jeffrey answered with a quizzical look on his face.

Jonathan saluted him. "Sir."

"Where's your dad, son?" Jeffrey's dad asked him.

"Sir, he's out back on the patio with my mom making barbecue, sir," Jonathan answered.

Jonathan remembers thinking nothing of seeing Jeffrey's dad. How he just thought of making better time on his wheelie.

A motorbike roar snaps Jonathan back into the present. He watches Elie pull into the driveway, jump off his bike and run up to Alex. Elie holds up his arms and receives a two-handed high-five followed by a playful punch to the chest; he blocks it, and throws her one back. Jonathan watches them punch and block one another until Elie seizes one of her gloves. She makes a halfhearted attempt to get loose but he pulls her in close.

Jonathan is pulled back into his reverie despite himself. He recalls Jeffrey's father running back to the driveway and scooping up his son as vividly as if he were seeing it before him now. He remembers the empathy he felt when Mr. Dalton gave Jeffrey a long hug, kissed his forehead, and promised to be back soon. Jeffrey didn't let a single tear fall as he watched his dad run back to his jeep, Jonathan recollects noticing.

"Come on, bet I can beat you this time," Jonathan said, popping a wheelie—trying to get his best friend's mind off his father's departure. "One …!" Jonathan yelled. Jeffrey jumped back on his bike. "Two … three!" Front tires in the air, both boys chanted, "One one thousand, two one thousand." Both still had their bikes upright on five. *I'm going to beat him!* Jonathan was sure. But his father hurried out, toting a duffle bag. Jonathan's heart sank hard along with his bike. "No! You just got back!" Jonathan yelled, jumping off his BMX. "You can't leave again!" He wrapped his arms around his father's waist and held him tight.

"I know, champ. I know," his father told him.

"No! Don't go with him!" Jonathan begged. "Please!"

"I have to, champ, this one's important."

*Not more important than me!* Jonathan wanted to scream.

"I'll be back before you know it." He hugged his son, pried himself free, and ran to the jeep.

"Daddy, don't go!" Jonathan chased the jeep down the street.

Jeffrey followed on his bike.

"He took him!" Jonathan yelled at Jeffrey. "Your dad took him!" Jonathan pushed Jeffrey down, started kicking the bike, and then his friend.

Tears stream down Jonathan's face as he watches Elie kiss Alex. *Your fault!* Jonathan sobs, glowering at Elie's black hair, thick brows, olive skin. *Your people's fault!* Jonathan squeezes his bat. He rubs the tears off his face, and steps out of the pick-up.

*** 

"You're so beautiful," Elie whispers. Alex smacks her lips on his. He closes his eyes and enjoys the moment. Then, suddenly feeling strangely anxious, he opens them and pulls away. He skims the shapes outside in the shadows, trying to locate the source of his discomfort.

"What is it?" she asks.

108

"Nothing," he tells her, feeling a little foolish. "Um, I've got to go finish packing. Later." He bolts to his bike.

"Wait!" Alex blurts out.

Elie turns, "What?"

"Come back after?" Alex lifts a brow suggestively.

Elie is surprised. "What about …?" He points to the ceiling.

"Mom took off this morning to see her sis up in Canada."

Elie grins. "Sweet … But I still have to pack."

"K. But come back." She points at the Buick. "We'll leave in my dad's car in the morning."

"Okay." Elie jumps on his bike and tries to kick-start it. It doesn't start. He tries a couple of times. "Oh, man. Not again."

"What's wrong?" Alex asks, and steps out of the garage.

Elie checks the spark plug and cocks his head. "It's loose." He gets off the bike and glances around.

Alex opens her mouth to speak but Elie quickly brings a finger to his pursed lips, and carefully circles the Buick. He shoots Alex a look, and mouths, "Weapons."

Alex scans a rake, shovel, metal garbage can. Elie shakes his head; nothing's behind the vehicle. He considers the separating hedge into the neighbor's front yard. Nothing. Alex gets a firm hold of a metal weed puller propped up against the wall.

"Hmm, I could have sworn I heard something," Elie says, and returns to the bike.

Alex laughs nervously.

"I must've not screwed it in tight enough," he says, and twists the spark plug in hard. He leans over the bike and gives her a soft kiss.

"See you in a bit," she says, eyes glistening, as he kicks the bike into gear.

***

Jeffrey is almost finished packing. Doris sits on his bed rubbing her bruised cheek, and watches Karen pull a sheet over a very dead Terry in *The Howling*.

"Still hurts?" Jeffrey asks.

"Two slaps in one day. What do you think?"

"I average at least two of something a day. Slaps. Punches." He touches his ribs. "Kicks. Sideburn yanking." He chuckles as he feels the side of his face. "Beer cans to the head." He tries to laugh as he runs his fingertips over the gash on his forehead but winces instead. "It's crazy what one can get used to."

110

"Or immune to," Doris sighs.

"You think werewolves become immune to the pain when they change?" He points at the TV.

On the screen, Eddie has come back from the dead. He quietly terrorizes Karen, plucks a bullet out of his forehead, throws his head back, and begins to transform.

"Eddie's going through nothing," Doris watches, eyes gleaming, "David from *London* goes through some serious shit. If I was a werewolf, I'd like to change just like David. More pain, more gain. It would send me out angrier. To go through all that … when I'd go out for the kill …" She contorts her fingers to resemble claws. "I'd tear them apart. Limb from limb. Devour their flesh, eat their souls."

"Oh, yeah? Here, have a leg," Jeffrey giggles, and hands her the drawing he sketched in class earlier.

"That's sick … I love it. Check this out!" Doris pulls her own sketchpad out of her knapsack. She flips it open.

"Wow! That is totally hot!" Jeffrey says, eyes gliding over the page.

"You think?"

"And the way she's holding him by the hair …" Mouth open, he hands her back the pad. "You're one scary girl, Doris Mitchell."

Their eyes meet and hold. Jeffrey lets out a nervous snort and his glasses slip down to the tip of his nose.

"Ha! Ha! You snarled!" Doris says, and snarls back.

Jeffrey snarls again, cheeks flushed.

"You're too cute," Doris tells him, pushing his glasses back up to the bridge of his nose.

\*\*\*

Scott turns off the convertible's headlights and slows.

Beside him, Jonathan shoots him a puzzled look.

"Check up ahead," Scott says, indicating the brown-paneled bungalow.

"The fuck we doing here?" Jonathan asks.

Backseat passengers, Lance and Ronald, lean forward to listen.

"Lookie, lookie," Scott wiggles his eyebrows at Jonathan and points up at Jeffrey's bedroom window, "the geeks sitting on the bed."

"So?" Jonathan sneers.

"Well, since you're pissed and I need to *take* a piss, I figure I could cheer you up, dude." Scott

112

downs the last of his beer, crushes the can and tosses it to Ronald. "Obama, give me one of those Trojans."

"What? No way," Ronald says, tapping his jacket. "I need these babies for this weekend."

"Just one, Mandingo," Scott teases.

Lance and Jonathan do their best to keep a straight face.

"Uh-uh," Ronald shakes his head. "They're staying in my pocket, my brother."

"Been in your pocket too long, bro," Scott continues. "Give me one before they expire."

Jonathan and Lance crack up.

"Fuck you." Ronald flips them the finger.

"C'mon bro, you know you're not going to get any with that girl. *You* know it, *I* know it, *the whole school* knows it," Scott needles, and fist bumps Lance.

"He's right, cuz," Lance adds. "Even though you're black, you got the bluest balls in town. That girl's going to make you bust a nut before she gives you a little somethin' somethin'." He throws Jonathan a wink.

"Why Mr. President," Jonathan says solemnly, "if you were ever accused by some chick of having unethical sexual relations, the whole fucking country would believe *you*."

"Oh, fuck you all!" Ronald whips Scott a condom.

***

Jeffrey and Doris sit on the bed, side by side, eyes on the television.

A thick ball of hamburger meat is slapped on a grill and gets squished down into a patty. *The Howling*'s end credits scroll up atop its sizzle.

"So you're really going to go?" Doris asks, still focused on the credits.

"Got no other option," Jeffrey answers, pretending to read the names.

"Even after what Jerkoff Johnson said was going to happen to us?"

*Come on, do it, chickenshit, do it.* Jeffrey moves his hand an inch closer to hers. "What do you want to do?"

"We could always run away," she says, moving her fingers closer to his.

*Did she move her fingers on purpose?* He feels his heart jump. "And … and go where?" he stutters.

Doris is silent.

"No, Warren's right. I have to go," Jeffrey tries to convince himself. "Stand up for myself. I can't let them push me around anymore. If my dad had it in him, maybe I do, too," he says, not daring to shift his gaze away from the screen.

"You *do* have it in you …," Doris says. "The way you stood up for me this morning …"

He takes a quick peek at her, and says, "I … I did nothing."

"You tried," she says. "That counts."

*Aww! She's laughing at me,* he figures, hurt. *She thinks I'm a pussy.* But then feels a finger caress his. "Well, they embarrassed you," he says boldly. "I had to. I should have done more." —He keeps his eyes on the credits, though— "But you shouldn't be embarrassed." Jeffrey sneaks a glance. "You *are* hot."

"What?" Doris squeezes his hand and turns to him, "Jeffrey Dalton did you check out my ass?"

Jeffrey tenses up, eyes glued to the floor. His face burns red.

"'Cause if you did, and think it's hot," Doris purrs, "then it's all right with me."

Jeffrey meets her gaze. She gives him a slight nod. He gulps hard. *Oh my God*, he thinks, ogling her mouth. *She wants to kiss me.* Jeffrey shivers, hesitates—*don't you chicken out now, geek*— and then lets the luscious purple gloss draw him in. His heart's pounding, his flesh feels on fire. Their lips meet … BAM! He receives a startling blow to his head. "What the fuck!"

Doris's face is soaked. She wipes it with her sleeve and inhales the acrid stench of the fluid. "It's piss!" she cries, then points at a condom scrap on the floor. "Someone took a leak in a fucking rubber and bombed it through the window," she screams. "Putrids! Putrids!"

"Touchdown!" Jonathan hoots outside, and honks three times, long and loud.

Jeffrey springs to the window. "I'll fucking kill them!" He digs his fingers into the sill and glares down.

Jonathan, standing on the convertible's passenger seat, holds Jeffrey's glare.

"Beer's on me, geek!" Scott shouts. "Just make sure you wrap your dick. I don't want your skank making me sick."

"Fuck, does he look pissed!" Ronald snorts.

"You have no fucking idea," Jeffrey utters through his teeth as the car peels off, tires squealing.

"You still think you'll be able to stand up to them?" Doris blubbers between sobs, pressing her bracelets into her temples.

"More than ever," Jeffrey says. He turns to her, "More than ever." He pulls her hands away from her head. "Come with me."

"Where?" She snivels.

Without answering, he leads Doris out of his room, down the hall, and into the master bedroom. Next to the four-poster bed, he stops. He opens the closet, reaches for the black army boots on the floor, and pulls a key out of the left one. "Hoo-ah!" he hollers, feeling his fury course through his veins. He pushes the hanging clothes out of the way.

"Is that a door?" she mutters—he can feel her trembling against his back.

Jeffrey slips the key in the lock. "Follow me."

Chapter 11

# DON'T THINK I DON'T KNOW WHO YOU ARE

A garage door rattles open. Sparrows, starlings, and blackbirds startle and call for the dawn. Elie and Alex, in camouflage coats, pants and boots, step into the crisp new day.

"Sorry, birdies," Alex says, as the flock flees its elm roost.

She slides the key into the lock, pops the Buick's trunk open, and they toss in their backpacks. Elie grins—he can't believe the glorious

118

night they've shared. *God, she's awesome*, he thinks for the hundredth time, and pulls her to him. They kiss.

"Mmm … mmm!" Alex tries to pull away.

Elie's eyes open and catch a peculiar reflection in Alex's wide-open, bulging eyes.

"Hey, Lover Boy!" Out of nowhere, four hooded, gloved and masked intruders— also in camouflage—seize them by the arms and try to force them into the open trunk.

"Alex!" Elie yells, and she manages to kick her assailant between the legs. Elie twists and punches himself free. "Inside!" he shouts, and they dart into the garage. But before they can reach the door to the house, Elie is tackled, and Alex is grabbed from behind.

Elie takes a hard punch to the stomach, jerks back, and bashes into his motorbike—parked next to the loveseat. He goes down in a daze and his bike falls on top of him.

The attacker squeezes Alex tight as he tries to drag her out of the garage. She smashes her foot down onto his, gives him a back kick and sends him into her punching bag. She steps forward and tries to spear hand the one who punched Elie. He side steps the blow and gives her a sweeping kick that knocks her off her feet.

119

"Leave her alone!" Elie hollers, pinned to the bike—he struggles to free his left boot caught between the front wheel and fender.

The aggressor jumps on top of Alex and punches her in the face, knocking her out. Another two come forward, grab her shoulders and legs, haul her to the car and toss her into the trunk.

With a sudden surge of adrenalin, Elie kicks the fender with the right, bending it back and setting his foot free. He scans the floor, grabs a fallen shovel, crawls to a stand and makes a dash for the Buick.

The four hostiles quickly surround him.

"Come on, fuckers! Let's see what you've got!" Elie swings the shovel menacingly, springs forward, but is met with a powerful kick to the ribs. With the air knocked out of his lungs, he drops his weapon.

They pounce on him instantly, hitting and kicking him as if *he* were the punching bag. Through the shower of blows, Elie spots an opening and pushes through. One assailant grabs him by the hair and throws him into the beefiest one, who headbutts him hard and sends him to the ground. He grabs Elie's arms, pulls him up, and drags him to the trunk.

"Motherfuckers, don't think I don't know who you are!" Elie stammers. "Lance!" He snarls, and manages to jerk one arm free in a futile attempt to claw the mask off. Another attacker comes up behind and pins Elie's arm back. "Come on, cuz," he gasps. "Don't do this."

The two attackers stop in front of the trunk, spin Elie around, and are about to force him.

"Come on—" Elie pleads, looking into their brown eyes, seeing the dark lids the masks cannot hide "—don't fall into this ... racial bullshit!"

The two attackers pause.

"Think about it," Elie sputters, "if they're calling me ... a fucking A-rab ... they must be calling you fucking—"

The third assailant boots Elie in the chest and sends him backwards halfway into the trunk. The fourth forces Elie all the way in, crushing him into Alex.

"Jonathan, Scott, Lance, Ronald?" Elie guesses. "I'm going to fucking kill you!" He pulls himself up and he gets a hard blow to the jaw. Blackness ensues.

*\*\*\**

One of the hostiles takes a roll of duct tape out of his pocket and tapes Elie's mouth and wrists first, then Alex's. Another frisks Elie, finds his phone, and pockets it. He searches and gropes Alex, pocketing her cell phone too.

The trunk is slammed shut, keys flung into the neighboring bushes. The garage door comes down. Four pairs of boots hit the pavement.

Chapter 12

# COME ON, EL-HAGE!
# COME ON, PETERSON!

The first rays of light barely peer over the horizon as a small yellow bus idles in the school's parking lot.

Behind the wheel, Sergeant O'Sullivan sports his Army Combat Uniform; nametag, rank and ARMY displayed on his serge. He checks the rearview mirror. The students sit quietly. *My misfits*, he thinks. A pool of camouflage. *No, my* unit, he tells himself, and begins to scan the row directly behind him.

*Dalton, you look like a man in your dad's fatigues,* he remarks to himself. *Hmm,* he chuckles, *Mitchell must be wearing five sweaters under that jacket.* He smiles inwardly: *they're here; mission accomplished.* Dawn has her earphones plugged in; *iPod, not on the list. Should I let her keep it? We'll see.* Cindy sleeps, head leaning back, open-mouthed, next to Sharon who's engrossed in *Twilight* by Stephenie Meyer. Heather and Ronald sit arm in arm behind them. Billy Bob sits alone, his boot up next to Ronald's ear, fidgeting with the heel. Stretched out in the last seat is Lance. *That boy's huge,* O'Sullivan thinks. Scott and Jonathan flank the right. *Willis, McCalla, Johnson,* the teacher counts, *my three alphas ... let's see who takes the lead.* George and Rosa are half-asleep in front of Scott and Jonathan. In front of the Latino couple is Kimberly, who appears rather sullen—her braids hang over her vacant stare—*in one of her moods, again*—sitting with Abigail. *Designer camouflage, Simmons? Little Miss Perfect. Hmm, that'll all change.* And Zack—*the actor*—who leans back against the window, feet poking out into the aisle. *Let's see how well he does out there ...* O'Sullivan smiles. *Well, there's always the USO ....* Then two empty seats in front of the boy.

*Sixteen out of eighteen.* He lets out a deep sigh. *Come on, El-Hage! Come on, Peterson!*

The students start protesting:

"Sir, how much longer, sir?"

"Sir, come on, sir."

"Sir, you said o six hundred, sir."

The Sarge glances at his watch. Already fifteen minutes behind schedule! He sweeps the area, reaches for the handle and pulls the doors closed. Some of the students applaud. Resigned, he throws the bus into gear and in the rearview catches Scott and Jonathan fist bump. He hits the brakes.

The students jerk forward—some almost fall out of their seats. O'Sullivan checks the side mirrors. Someone's coming up behind the bus.

Jonathan swings around. "Shit, who's that?"

"I can't tell," Lance says. "Too dark."

"It's only a jogger, dude," Scott says.

O'Sullivan shrugs off his disappointment and drives off.

"All right you bunch of misfits," he belts, "let's hear it. From the top: SURVIVAL!"

The entire class begins to monotonously recite: "S - Size up the situation, surroundings, physical condition, equipment."

In his mirror, he can see Dawn silently watching the others.

"I can't hear you!" he shouts, trying to wake the students from their near-comatose state.

"U - Use all your senses," they shout a little louder. "R - Remember where you are."

"Louder!" the Sarge demands.

"V - Vanquish fear and panic," they now yell. "I - Improvise and improve."

"Louder!"

"V - Value living," they boom in unison. "A - Act like the natives."

The bus passes a huge placard: VOTE CHARLES M. COLLINS FOR MAYOR. The students roar; rooting, fist bumping, high-fiving, patting Ronald. Some start hollering Native war cries.

O'Sullivan bellows, "L!"

"Live by your wits!" the students finish off.

O'Sullivan smiles, satisfied. *My* unit!

***

The Buick's trunk lock pops out and the lid swings open. Elie, drenched with sweat, jumps out of the claustrophobic, ravaged interior, survival knife at-the-ready. "Clear," he gasps. "No one here." He helps pull out a sopping Alex.

She gulps for air, and wipes perspiration from her eyes. "You sure?"

He scans the quiet neighborhood and spots the jimmied trunk lock on the asphalt—the keys are no longer in the slot. Across the street, a curtain moves. "Fuck!" he cries. *Was someone watching the whole time?* He lets out a fierce and deafening roar: the veins on his forehead seem ready to explode. Alex falters and leans against the car, touching her swollen jaw. Elie examines her wounds in the twilight. Bruises on her face and neck. He winces.

"It's that bad?" she asks.

"Fuckers!" he curses, and opens his mouth but stifles a scream, making his features appear darker, almost monstrous. His thick brows furrow together. He pounds his fists on the hood of the car.

Alex cups his beaten jaw in her shaking hands. "It's okay, baby. It's okay. We'll get them."

"You better fucking believe it," he tells her and digs into his pockets. "They've got my phone."

"Mine too," she says, feeling her pockets.

Elie's face suddenly lights up. "Your laptop!"

Alex stares at him blankly.

He darts to the garage door. "We can track my phone's GPS!"

Chapter 13

# ON A FAMILIAR COUNTRY ROAD

The school bus chugs up a steep hill. Students are half-asleep or already sleeping, others secretly text or play games on their cell phones. Scott stretches his neck. Jonathan, on his right, is dozing soundly. To his left, Lance is busy reading the *Hooper Times'* sports pages. *Man*, Scott lifts himself a few inches off his seat, *my ass is killing me*—it's been a long hour. He notices a gray spot on the black rubber runner—gum—and searches down the aisle for more things to distract him. Halfway down, a pair

128

of feet in grey socks wiggle. He looks up: Zack makes faces, and blows Kimberly kisses. *Fucking clown*, Scott thinks, *he's wasting his time. That bitch is always depressed.* He smiles to himself. *I can give her something to be happy about*, he thinks, grabbing his crotch. He looks over at Abigail, who runs her fingers through her hair and seems to be looking for her reflection in the window. *Hmm*—he runs his fingers under his shirt, up his chiseled abs, and rubs his chest—*I'd love to mess up that blond mop*, he thinks, and shifts his sights to Doris, sitting behind O'Sullivan. *Skank …?* He props his arms on the seat in front of him and studies her for a long moment: The way her curls dangle in the ponytail. Her small ears. The smooth line of her profile. The dark facade. *Nah, you're beautiful.* He leans back into his seat, locks his fingers behind his head, *Only thing skanky about you is … you fucked your mother's boyfriend.*

"Hey," Zack says, pointing at the window. "Hope!"

Scott looks out and spots a sign, NEXT EXIT HOPE.

Zack continues, "That's the place—"

"With those crazy kids from the club," Billy Bob cuts him off, shouting from the back.

The bus reaches the top of the hill.

Lance leans on Billy Bob's seat. "Yeah, it was on the radio … something about two teens kicking the shit out of everyone."

George turns in his seat. "They said they were on some kind of a super drug or something like that," he tells Lance.

"Yeah," Scott says, and pokes George's bulky chest, "some of you guys need super drugs to be tough guys like us guys." He fist bumps Lance.

"You know," Lance says.

Scott looks down the aisle wondering if he got Doris's attention and catches a glance at the rearview. O'Sullivan smiles at him with a twinkle in his eyes.

The roaring sound of a motorcycle approaches the bus from behind.

Jonathan, Scott, and Lance spin in their seats and peer out the back door's window.

"It couldn't be," Jonathan blurts out.

"No way," Scott punches Jonathan's arm, aiming to knock the shock out of him.

"The fuck," Jonathan says, countering with a backhand to Scott's chest. "Then what's that?" Jonathan points at a motorcycle appearing at the top of the hill.

Scott squints. "I can't make it out."

"It's a sport bike," Ronald says hovering over Billy Bob's seat. "Not his."

Scott smacks Jonathan's back. "See?"

"Whose?" Heather asks.

"No one's," Ronald answers.

"Oh, man, I think it's a chick!" Scott says. The biker looks up. "Check out the sexy MILF!" he hollers.

Ronald and George both stand to get a better look but their girlfriends pull them back.

Skin-tight black leather and curves—*Call me a motherfucker*, Scott thinks, and watches her cruise up right behind them. She veers as if to pass, but stays alongside the bus. She smiles at the boys in the back row. "She's flirting us, dudes!" Scott announces, puffing up like a strutting peacock. He jumps into Billy Bob's seat, pushes past him, and pounds the window. "Wooo, hooo!"

"McCalla, sit your ass down!" O'Sullivan yells.

"Now that's what I'm talking about," Scott says, ogling. He notices her slim thighs squeezing the gas tank—the letters D-I-L-L-Y painted fire-red on the metal.

The woman zips her jacket up beneath her chin.

Scott tries to rile up the boys. "Whoa, she just flashed me her tits!"

Billy Bob and Lance press against the windows.

She leans into her bike—her pink thong rises over her pants.

Billy Bob, Lance, and Scott cheer, howl, and stomp their feet.

"Now, that's spanky," Scott says, watching her ride ahead and nod to his teacher as he gives her the right of way. What a fuckin' sexy ass! The image of her thong disappears behind a bend, leaving him staring at a sign: NEXT EXIT CROSBY, 30 MILES.

***

The bright morning sun promises another beautiful day, O'Sullivan thinks. A tall neon sign flickers off in the distance—EATS ALL NIGHT – 24HR. He smacks his lips. He can almost taste it. Can almost hear his father scolding him and his brother, Brian, as they fight over the mouthwatering brownie they're supposed to share.

*"Daddy, Timmy's eating all the cream," Brian cries.*

*"O'Sullivan, you leave some for your little brother," their father commands.*

*"Sir, yes, sir."*

*"And you," their father points at Brian, "stop being a wimp."*

132

Another sign is coming up on the opposite side of the road. O'Sullivan slows the bus, makes a sharp left, and heads straight for the forest, passing alongside: NEXT EXIT, HOPE, 27 MILES.

Lance, Scott, and Sharon jump to their feet, "Sir, what are you doing, sir?"

O'Sullivan doesn't pay attention to them. The bus tramples through brush.

"*Dios mio!*" Rosa cries out. "He's going to kill us!"

"Hang on!" Zack yells, clutching the seat in front of him.

O'Sullivan drives the bus through thick branches, and then bumps along a narrow mountain path huddled with trees.

"Fuck me," Billy Bob mumbles, placing his hands on his head.

All the kids turn to look at one another.

## Chapter 14

# ALRIGHT, SOLDIERS, THIS IS IT

O'Sullivan catches the students mouthing to each other in his rearview mirror. *Impressed and spooked,* he thinks. *Good combo.*

"This is where my father brought me for my first survival weekend," he shouts over the hum and bustle of the bus. "I was thirteen. I was left alone for forty-eight hours with even less than what you soldiers have with you today." The bus bounces over a rut. "I spent most of that first day trying to find a way out of here. By nightfall, at the

134

sound of the first howl, I climbed a tall tree and hid there."

"Sir, was it a wolf, sir?" Rosa asks.

"Cold, scared and with nothing more than a canteen of water to fill the emptiness in my gut."

"Oh, sir, how could your father do that to you, sir?" Sharon exclaims.

"Now, I don't know what got into me," O'Sullivan continues, "but before dawn, I found myself back on ground level and, knowing that that son of a bitch of an old man of mine wasn't coming back for me for another twenty-four hours, I started to take control of my situation." He veers the bus sharply to the left to dodge a pothole.

"Sir, you got guts, sir!" George praises.

"I carved a long branch into a spear and got busy fishing and hunting—eating raw food so I could save the two matches in my kit for warmth that night." O'Sullivan scans their faces: They listen, perched on the edge of their seats. "By nightfall, I had lost all sense of fear. I sat in front of my fire listening to a chorus of loons and coyotes, clutching my spear, waiting for the worst." Branches scrape the side of the bus, startling the kids. "But the beauty of the flames was too mesmerizing and before I knew it, I woke to the warmth of the sun on my face. And, as I was thanking the good Lord, I felt a shadow upon me. I looked up and there he was, my father, the man who gave me the balls"—O'Sullivan pulls a medal out of his front pocket and holds it up so every student can see—"that would lead me to this."

The teens gasp at the sight of the Purple Heart.

"Hoo-ah!" Scott and Billy Bob whisper loudly.

Driving with one hand, and holding his medal up with the other, O'Sullivan studies his charges through the rearview mirror, waiting for more.

"Hoo-ah!" Scott, Billy Bob, George, Lance, and Ronald cheer.

"Hoo-ah!" they all chant—except for Dawn.

*Way to go, O'Sullivan,* he boasts. *Even Dalton and Mitchell have joined in.*

Ten minutes later, O'Sullivan slows the bus to a stop and swings the door open. He stands, leans into his cane and turns to his students.

"Alright, soldiers, this is it. This is where you leave everything you can't take with you. Your fears, your problems, your animosities all have to stay on the bus. We are now one unit. We must all work together and follow the eight simple rules. Anything not on the list shall remain on the bus."

He notices Jeffrey and Doris share a glance.

He places his cane behind his seat, and continues, "Or there will be consequences. Anybody caught with anything prohibited will receive demerit points. Yes, that's right, I will be marking you. I will be watching you at all times. Those who think they can defy me will fail the class. Am I clear?" No one speaks. "I can't hear you."

"Sir, yes, sir!"

"Now let's move it," O'Sullivan orders.

The students jump to their feet. Jeffrey swings his backpack over his head, knocking off his camouflage print cap.

O'Sullivan spots the cut over the teen's eye. "What happened to your head, son?"

"Sir, I ran into a branch, sir," Jeffrey answers.

"A branch?"

"Sir, yes, sir."

The boys in the back chuckle.

O'Sullivan glowers at them while speaking to Jeffrey. "A lot more branches out here, son. Got to be careful. You just make sure, if one comes at you out of nowhere, you nip it before it clips you." The Sarge gives Jeffrey a curt nod. "You follow?"

"Sir, yes, sir," Jeffrey answers, and nods back.

"Good." O'Sullivan grabs his backpack and hobbles off the bus, leaving his cane behind.

Some of the kids take food, electronics, and make-up out of their backpacks and place them under their seats. Dawn stashes her iPod in one of her uniform's many pockets. One after the other, the students exit the bus.

Though cooler, the Indian summer reaches into the secluded forest. The teens don camouflage toques, caps, hats, and gloves, breathe in the clean air, and take in their surroundings. Even with the thick bed of brittle leaves on the ground, the dense vegetation makes it difficult to see very far. O'Sullivan appears from behind a tree, walking over with the help of a long branch. "Ssh!" he hisses. "What do you hear?"

Rosa pulls her wool cap off her ear. "Birds?" she asks.

O'Sullivan shakes his head.

"The wind," George blurts out.

O'Sullivan frowns impatiently.

"Sir, George breaking wind, sir!" Ronald shouts, sniffing the air.

The kids burst with laughter.

"Come on, soldiers!" The Sarge hollers. "Say it: U!"

"Use all your senses!" they chant.

"Now use 'em!"

They listen carefully.

"Oh, oh, oh … Sir, water, sir!" Billy Bob exclaims.

"Right!" O'Sullivan exhales. "Now lead us to that water, Jenkins."

"Sir, yes, sir!" Billy Bob slips on his backpack and heads for the water. "You heard The Sarge, now follow the leader, you bunch of misfits!"

O'Sullivan grins watching his unit push and snap branches to create their own path in the untamed forest. When Jonathan skirts by him, he reaches out, grabs his backpack, and pulls him close.

"Sir?" Jonathan asks.

"What happened to Dalton's head?"

"Sir, you heard him, the geek's blind, sir."

"The geek? You're lucky 'the geek' is not a rat, otherwise I'd send your ass home right now."

"Sir, I swear I had nothing to do with it, sir."

"From here on, you and your buddies are to lay off Dalton. Even better, I want you to make nice with him."

"Sir, you know I can't stand him. If it wasn't for his father, *my* father would be …," Jonathan's eyes well.

"Oh, don't tell me you're going to cry again." O'Sullivan stretches his arms out wide. "You want another hug? Here? In front of your buddies?"

139

Jonathan bows his head.

"Your father made his own choice; nobody twisted his arm. So lay off. You hear me?"

Jonathan remains silent.

O'Sullivan takes a step forward, "Did. You. Hear. Me?"

The slender teen looks up at him, and, jaw clenched, answers, "Sir, yes, sir."

"Now move along."

Jonathan starts off.

"And Johnson?"

Jonathan stops, his back to The Sarge.

"I'd better not find out you had anything to do with El-Hage and Peterson not showing."

Chapter 15

# DON'T WANT YOU TURNING JUST YET

The group stands at the bed of an olive-tinted stream, bordered by dense clumps of five-foot tall cattails.

"Too cool," Rosa says. "It's transparent. I can see the stones at the bottom."

O'Sullivan tugs a couple of cattails out by the base and shakes them clean in the icy water. He peels back the pale brown stalk of one, revealing a long white core, and bites into it.

141

"Yuck!" Abigail squeals, crinkling her nose.

O'Sullivan chews as he speaks. "Besides their nutritional value how are these plants imperative for your survival?"

The students look to one another for answers.

O'Sullivan pulls a knife out from his utility belt and shaves the other stalk's root. He whips it into the air and all watch it land inches from Scott's feet.

Scott pulls the cattail from the ground and is impressed by the sharpness of the tip.

"Sir, I get it, I get it, sir!" Zack exclaims. "You can make arrows." He yanks a cattail out from its root, too.

Heather also reaches out for one and squeezes the seven-inch, dark brown pollen head; the golden fluff dances in the warm breeze. "And pillows, sir."

"And fire starter. Very good, Schwartz, very good, Williams," O'Sullivan says.

The students begin to collect cattails.

"Whoa, whoa, slow down," The Sarge commands. "Leave them for now. You can collect those later. First things first. Take out your empty bottles."

"Sir, my bottles are full, sir," Kimberly says with a smile.

"Mine too," Abigail drawls.

Most of the kids confirm the same.

"No problem. Empty them."

Kimberly asks, "Sir, empty, sir?"

"Empty," the teacher says, brusquely.

"Did he say empty?" Rosa asks Heather.

"Empty?" The group asks one another.

"Empty!" O'Sullivan shouts.

The stream babbles. A chipmunk darts by.

Sharon shakes her head. "Sir, you want me to dump this clean water, sir?"

"What am I, on mute? I said empty! Now!" He paws the ground with his boot.

Most of the students have two one-quart bottles. The ones with full bottles pour the water to the ground.

O'Sullivan turns to Doris, "Is that a two-quart canteen, Mitchell?"

"Sir, yes, sir."

"I like that." He flashes his identical canteen. "Go ahead. I want you to be the first. Go on, stick your canteen in the stream."

Scott's emerald eyes glimmer as he watches Doris pull off a glove, bend, and fill her canteen in the water. He fondles his arrow. There's a croak and he looks down; a toad is puffed up by his feet. He swiftly places his foot on top of it. And holds it there.

Doris raises the canteen to her lips.

"Uh uh, not yet," O'Sullivan tells her. *Okay, time to pull out the big guns,* he decides. "Legend has it," he says, "that werewolves would go through metamorphosis after drinking from certain enchanted streams."

Jeffrey and Doris exchange a glance—how does he know this?

"So, we must first purify the water," O'Sullivan explains. "Don't want you changing into a werewolf," he says, with a wink. He pulls out one of many pill bottles from a bagful in his backpack—the label reads: WATER PURIFICATION TABLETS —uncaps it, and hands Doris two turquoise tablets. "One tablet per quart and let stand for thirty minutes. Drink sparingly, soldiers. That's all you're getting 'til tomorrow. Next."

Jeffrey has a two-quart canteen similar to Doris's. He dunks it in the stream and the others follow suit.

O'Sullivan pours a handful of tablets into his hand, sets the pill bottle on a boulder, and goes around dropping tablets into all the students' canisters. Dawn holds out two plastic water bottles, arms outstretched. A huge grin lights up her pale face. O'Sullivan drops a tablet into each bottle, and pats her head. *Sweetie*, he thinks, and continues. When he reaches Zack, a duck quacks and takes wing behind the nearby cattails. The boy screams. The girls echo with shrieks. The others jump. An unflinching O'Sullivan frowns. *You just screamed like a girl, boy,* O'Sullivan scoffs inwardly, looking at Zack, who's unable to meet his gaze. *No worries, we just might be able to fix that.* The Sarge drops a tablet into each of Zack's bottles.

George picks up the pill container resting on the boulder and reads the label aloud: "side effects such as chest pain, cyanosis, conjunctivitis, headache, muscle pull and diarrhea."

"Diarrhea! Ugh!" the girls groan.

O'Sullivan grabs the bottle out of George's hand and tosses it into his backpack. "Only if used in *excess*."

"Sir, speaking of diarrhea," Billy Bob asks, "what do we use for toilet paper, sir?"

"S!" The Sarge hollers, strapping on his backpack.

All except for Dawn chant, "Size up the situation, surroundings, physical condition, equipment."

O'Sullivan indicates the many fallen leaves.

"Oh, no!" Billy Bob complains.

145

"You've got to be kidding," Cindy hisses, and separates her platinum bob into two ponytails.

"You need to focus on what you have and not what you want. Where you are and where you're going." O'Sullivan points at the mountaintop ahead. The unit gathers around him.

"Oh, my Lord!" Abigail lilts, putting a hand to her forehead.

Ronald surveys the landscape. "Sir, that's a long climb, sir."

"Wow! That's beautiful," Rosa sighs. "*Que hermoso*."

"My feet are going to kill me," Kimberly moans. "I don't think I can make it all the way up there."

Lances nudges Billy Bob. "Now *that's* high."

O'Sullivan focuses on the long rise of fir greens mixed with browns contrasted against the wide-open blue sky. *Breathtaking*, he marvels.

*\*\*\**

Dawn peers over the teacher's head, taking in the mountainside, as she slowly joins the group. Her stomach flutters. She's giddy. *I can climb that*, she tells herself, and out of the corner of her eye, she spies a gloved hand snatch one of the pill bottles from O'Sullivan's backpack. She curtains her eyes, but peeks through her fingers.

146

"All righty then. Let's move it!" The Sarge orders, and a kind of marching begins.

Scott brushes past Dawn to catch up to the unit. He gives her a charming smile, and she feels a chill shoot down the length of her spine. Without knowing why, she snaps a glance over her shoulder and notices a cattail arrow stabbed into the ground—something shiny glints at the bottom of it. She takes a few steps toward it, and her eyes widen. A toad. *Dead!* Eyes bulging, with the arrow pierced right through its center. *Why would Scott do that?* she wonders, sadly.

## Chapter 16

# THIRSTY? DAMN, YOU?

It is a steep hill. All struggle with the dewy terrain and the weight of their backpacks.

Billy Bob stops. "Yo, check it," he tells the kids behind him and—like Dorothy in the *Wizard of Oz*—knocks his heels together. "Ta-dah!" he exclaims, lifting his right foot to show off the one-inch spiked cleats. "See? Just like that!" he flaunts, and sprints effortlessly up the hill to fall in behind O'Sullivan, who maintains a healthy lead.

The last stretch of the climb is particularly challenging. O'Sullivan grabs at protruding tree roots to pull himself up and extends his staff for Billy Bob to take hold of. Billy Bob grasps it with one hand and reaches for his sister's hand with the other. Sharon takes it and reaches for Cindy's. The unit forms a chain. When Doris takes Scott's hand, Cindy gives him a sharp push, ramming Doris into Jeffrey. Scott pulls Doris up.

"Thanks," she says, and in the same moment Jeffrey tumbles. "Jeffrey!" she yells.

Jeffrey claws at the earth but inertia pulls him down the slope. No one attempts to help, then Jonathan, last in line, seizes Jeffrey's backpack. "Here," he says, "take my hand."

"No thanks." Jeffrey curls his lip and starts up again—eyes on Doris holding Scott's hand.

Impressed, The Sarge gives Jonathan a curt nod.

"What up with that, Obama?" Lance asks Ronald.

"The fuck I know," he replies, wiping his neck with his shirt collar. "Maybe J.J.'s going geek on us."

"Uh uh, he's up to something," Lance says, slipping his fingers under his toque to scratch his smooth scalp.

149

One by one, the students clamber over the crest and raise their arms in victory; they have conquered this stretch of mountain. They take a moment to catch their breaths. Some sit on rocks or decaying, fallen logs. They pull off damp gloves and wipe their faces with sweaty hats.

Sharon ties her jacket around her waist. "I am dying of thirst," Sharon pants, pulling out her water bottle.

"Me too!" Rosa huffs, raising her water bottle. "Cheers."

Abigail wrinkles her nose.

"Mmm, it's delicious," Rosa says.

Abigail leans in. "Are you kidding?"

"No, really. It's refreshing." Rosa takes another swallow. "Chilly cool. Puts a drench to my quench."

Abigail takes a swig from her own bottle. "Mmmm," she moans between gulps.

Billy Bob sticks his tongue out. "Yuck!" He shakes his head at the sight of the girls drinking the stream water and walks toward Lance, who has just re-emerged from behind a bush, zipping up his pants. Lance licks his dry lips and winces. "Thirsty?" Billy Bob asks.

"Damn. You?" Lance utters.

"Like the A-rab's camel." Billy Bob pulls his water bottles out of his coat. "But there's no way I'm drinking this crap."

"Don't worry, I'm packing." Lance looks around and—seeing The Sarge is busy talking to Zack—sneaks a beer can out from one of his jacket pockets. He cracks it open, muffling the sound with his coat sleeve, and takes a swig. They fist bump.

"Good," Billy Bob says, pouring out his water, "'cause I got this fear of having to wipe my butt with them leaves."

"You know." Lance hands Billy Bob the beer.

"Got poison ivy doing that once."

"Shit!" Lance says, with a snort. "Bet you'll never do that again."

Billy Bob is about to take a swig but—hearing footsteps behind him—hides the can.

"Just Scott," Lance tells him, watching Scott strut back toward the mountain's edge.

\*\*\*

Jonathan is the last to crest the mountain. He turns to look down the slope.

"Hey, J.J." Scott walks up behind him.

"Wow, that's fucking steep," Jonathan says. "Wouldn't you love to hit that on skis?"

"What's up with the geek?" Scott asks him.

151

Jonathan wipes the back of his hand across his forehead. "Sarge wants us to lay off or else."

"And you're going to listen?" Scott says, raising his upper lip and creasing his brow as he pulls out his water bottle.

Jonathan grins.

"Ha! Ha! ... What you got in mind?" Scott asks, and quenches his thirst.

Jonathan wiggles his eyebrows and digs into his pocket but stops short, turning his head. "You hear that?"

"What?" Scott asks.

"Motorcycle."

"Where?" Scott pricks up his ears and looks around. "I don't hear it."

After a moment, Jonathan points down the mountainside. "There," he says.

The hum of a motor echoes faintly in the distance.

"Oh, yeah," Scott says. "It's coming from the road. Must be that MILF zooming back to flash those titties at me again."

Jonathan is silent a moment, then looks at Scott. "What if it's them?"

"Who?" Scott asks, and then rolls his eyes. "Chillax, man. It'll take them forever to get out of that trunk and they have no way of calling for help." He pats his pockets.

"Yeah, you're probably right. You'd better get rid of those phones," Jonathan says.

"I thought I'd sell them." Scott pulls the phones out.

"What are you, stupid? The Sarge finds them—" Jonathan sees that one of the phones' screens is flashing. "Look! GPS on!" he points to it.

"Shit!" Scott flings the phones down the mountain.

"What did you do that for?" Jonathan cries. "They're still on! The A-rab's going to find us!"

"Fuck!" Scott realizes and starts downhill.

"Forget it. You'll never find them," Jonathan yells after him.

"Bah," Scott waves a hand. "They probably smashed, anyways."

Jonathan scans the hill. "Let's just hope."

***

One phone has landed beside a thorny sapling, right side up, screen lit, GPS mode on.

Chapter 17

# THE CLEARING

It's nearing noon when O'Sullivan leads his pack through thicker forest. Using branches, knives, and their arms, the group whacks through tall shrubs and clumps of fir trees. It's colder in the high mountain shade, but it doesn't seem to affect the unit. They are gung-ho, O'Sullivan thinks with a smile, thrusting their way through the wilderness.

O'Sullivan stops. The troop stops, poised in mid-whack, and wait on him for the go-ahead.

154

"Don't look at me," he says. "I've already aced this class."

They pan their surroundings.

"The thicket's too dense here," Sharon remarks.

"It's a dead end," Zack affirms.

Billy Bob checks to his left. "It's all downhill from here," he adds.

George ruffles some bushes and a couple of chokecherries patter to the ground. "Nowhere to go from here either," he shouts.

"Anybody?" Zack asks. "Anything?"

They glance at one another and shake their heads. They turn to The Sarge.

"S!" he hollers.

"Size up the situation, surroundings, physical condition, equipment," the unit chants and begins to scatter, searching thoroughly through different parts of the brush.

A few minutes later, Zack yells, "Hey, a rabbit!" The small animal scampers through the brush. "Over here!" he yells, following quickly after it, pushing his way through the foliage. The others, including O'Sullivan, rush over and follow him through. They step into a clearing, startling a raccoon that hisses and bares its teeth at them. Lance and Billy Bob jump back, but the others are

155

unfazed. O'Sullivan darts toward it and the raccoon scurries off. He turns to Lance and Billy Bob, forehead wrinkled, "R!"

Lance and Billy Bob are speechless.

"Remember where you are!" the others bark at them.

"As you can see," O'Sullivan says, "you'll come across plenty of animals out here. And if you show *them* no fear, they will fear *you*."

He leads his students into the clearing. *My sheep*, he thinks.

*\*\*\**

"Check it out guys," Rosa says twirling, stepping over rotting branches and crunching pinecones with her boots. "It's a perfect circle."

"The air's warmer up here," Heather says.

Ronald slips off his cap. "Yeah," he says, looking up. "No more trees. I can finally feel the sun!" He runs his hand over his trim, wiry hair.

"It's beautiful," Sharon says as she kicks up some multicolored leaves.

"Sir, is this where we're camping, sir?" Jonathan asks.

O'Sullivan nods.

Kimberly sets her backpack down and sighs. "Finally!"

"Whoa, that's some fire pit," George says, indicating the huge area circled off by stones that nestles the remnants of burnt logs at the center point.

"Big enough to barbeque us a moose," Scott says. "Or a Latin Pitbull." He yanks off George's cap and rubs his buzz cut.

"Grrr." George flexes his muscles.

"Speaking of, sir," Lance says, patting his belly, "when are we going to eat, sir?"

"Yeah, sir, when do we eat, sir?" the others echo.

"Alright, alright, you've all earned it, soldiers. You did well out there!" The Sarge praises. "We're going to split up into two groups. One group is staying here to set up camp. The other is coming fishing with me. Who wants to fish?"

Several hands fly up, including Jeffrey, Doris, Dawn, and Sharon's.

"Jenkins?" O'Sullivan blurts. "I thought you were a vegan?"

"Sir, yes, but all of a sudden I've got a craving for raw fish, sir," Sharon replies, a small line creasing her brow.

"Not just fish, but raw. I like that, Jenkins. Find me my stream. Hoo-ah!"

"Hoo-ah!" the troop cries out.

***

Zack sits on a thick log in front of the pit and counts the students around him. Circling the pit chewing charred fish-on-a-stick in front of the small fire, some are also sitting on logs while others sit on boulders. A few collect firewood that they place next to a large pile of cattails along the periphery. *Sixteen.* Zack then counts the green or brown one-person pup tents that form a circle around them. *Sixteen? Hmm!* He is puzzled. *Where's his tent*, he thinks, looking across the pit at O'Sullivan, crouched on one knee busily stripping a yew branch. Zack considers him a moment then concludes, *I'll bet he's going to sleep out under the stars or maybe on a tree branch. Yeah!* He chuckles to himself and gets up to collect the driest, hardest cattail stems from the pile. He cuts off the tops and hands them to Abigail sitting on a boulder next to him. "Here," he says, squeezing the heads, "you can use the plastic bag from your survival kit to make pillows."

"Great idea," Abigail says, chewing on trout, "lucky I thought of it," she teases, nudging Zack playfully. She pulls the bag out from her kit in front of her and begins to stuff it, sneezing when fluff finds its way into her nose.

"Bless you!" Kimberly says, taking some cattail heads from Zack to fill her own plastic bag.

Zack grabs the half dozen cattail stems he's collected and crosses to O'Sullivan.

A few feet away, Scott shaves the end of a long branch with his army knife. "I bet I make the first kill, Hollywood," Scott announces aloud to Zack, holding up his crude spear.

Zack looks over and catches Dawn, water bottle to her lips, shifting her sparkling eyes from Scott to him. *She wants me to respond,* Zack grins. *How cute.* "I don't know about that," Zack replies, surprised he's bothering to answer, "wouldn't be fair. I've had some great training." He kneels beside the teacher and begins to sharpen his stems. "I'd just be taking your money."

"Shut up!" Scott snarls. "I was hunting and killing while you were still peeing your bed, son." He looks over at Jonathan, "Speared my first cottontail when I was ten years old. Right, J.J.?"

Zack looks over at Jonathan, but Jonathan doesn't respond. His face seems frozen in an ugly grimace as he watches Sharon chew on a cattail root. She picks up another root and rubs it clean. "Here, try it." She offers it to him. "It's delicious."

"Yuk, no way." Jonathan waves his hand and reaches for his canteen.

Billy Bob grabs the stalk from his sister's hand, springs up and pretends that the roots are attacking. "Aaaahh!" he cries, "Alien!" and almost steps on Scott. *Silly guy*, Zack thinks, *so way over-the-top.*

Scott releases a ninja battle cry and jumps to his feet. "*Hitokiri*," he yells.

"Prepare to die, Kung Fu Panda!" Billy Bob shouts, crouching into a defensive stance—his ginger locks bounce atop his sun-kissed freckles. He and Scott put on a show, battling with spear and cattail.

Eyes glued to the scene, Zack drops his arrow-making and is about to join the scene when O'Sullivan holds out his palm. *Oh, right … the bow,* Zack reminds himself. He digs into his survival kit, pulls out the fishing line, and hands it to The Sarge. The teacher tightens the line around the notched tips of the stripped yew branch and explains the process, though Zack finds it difficult to pay attention as his eyes flit back to the scene, wishing he were up there putting on the show.

Billy Bob catches the spear in his armpit. "Ahhhh! … I have taught you well, Asshopper," he croaks in an Asian accent, and dies a long, dramatic death. The group, in stitches, applauds.

Zack leaps to his feet, "Bravo! Bravo!" He claps the loudest.

*****

Twilight. The kids chat around the crackling campfire, enjoying the fragrant smoke. Scott appears from behind the brush—one hand behind his back—and walks up to Doris. "I killed this one just for you," he whispers, and holds out his spear—a bloody white rabbit is pierced through it. "You want it?" he asks her.

Cindy saunters over and caresses the dead animal. She gets a hold of its paw, smiles at Scott, and slashes the rabbit's foot off with one swoop of her knife.

"Ouch!" a few of the boys hiss, grabbing themselves.

O'Sullivan comes up behind, followed by Zack, who drops a half dozen dead rabbits at the foot of the fire. "Ta dah!" Zack boasts holding out his arms, calling for praises.

The students clap and whistle. Zack bows like a great theater actor and wiggles his eyebrows at Scott. "Speech, speech," the group demands.

"Thank you, thank you, thank you," he begins. "First of all, I'd like to thank Mr. Stevens for believing in me and giving me the lead in Robin Hood. Second, Mr. Davis for teaching me how to

161

make it real by giving me intensive archery lessons, and lastly but mostly, I'd like to thank … me."

The group hoots and cheers.

O'Sullivan bangs his staff several times against a rock. "Today was a picnic. Tomorrow's the real challenge," he declares. "I want all of you to get plenty of rest. Finish off all remaining food. Do not leave anything out. Repeat. Do not leave anything out. You've got supper, water and warmth." He shakes his head. "I'm making this trip too easy for you." He holds his staff out like Moses parting the Red Sea. "Now remember, I want no screwing around … I will be watching." He slings his backpack over his shoulder.

"Sir, where are you going, sir?" Billy Bob gets to his feet, as do the rest.

"Shhh!" O'Sullivan hushes, waving his staff. "Listen."

The trees rustle, the students turn. A deer stands frozen before them.

"Look at that," Rosa whispers. "So cute. Like Bambi."

Scott pulls the spear out of his rabbit. "Watch this, Hollywood." He brings back his weapon and takes aim. "One shot," he whispers.

"Just like in *The Deer Hunter*," Zack says. He loads an arrow into his bow and also takes aim.

162

Eyes fixed on the deer, the kids—including Dawn—hold their breath and wait to see which one of the boys will kill it.

Branches snap. The deer bolts. Lance and Billy Bob jump back.

The rest of the unit charges into the woods to look for what scared the animal.

Lance and Billy Bob search the clearing.

"Where'd The Sarge go?" Billy Bob says.

"Sarge!" Lance calls out.

An engine roars. Trampling. Rumbling. The noise resonates between the trees.

Billy Bob and Lance grab on to each other's arms.

The students run back into the clearing.

"What was that?" Jonathan shouts, pushing through shrubs.

Lance lifts his shoulders. "I ... I think it was a motorbike."

Jonathan turns to Scott.

"Noooo ... don't even go there. Impossible," Scott says through his teeth. He turns to Billy Bob and Lance, "Where's the Sarge?"

They shake their heads. "I don't know," Billy Bob tells him.

The sound of the engine travels up the mountainside.

"It's The Sarge," Scott says with a grin, "he took off on us."

"He left?" Zack says.

"*Hijo de puta*!" George cries out. "Just like his old man did to him when he was kid."

"We're on our own," Rosa shouts.

Jonathan looks at Scott, then at Jeffrey.

Jeffrey and Doris exchange a glance.

"This is his test," Ronald says.

"He thinks he's going to scare us," Heather cries.

Rosa bellows, "*Coraje*!" as though she were leading them into battle.

Sharon shoots her arms into the air. "V!"

"Vanquish fear and panic!" the kids shout. "I! Improve and improvise …" They get louder as they continue down the list.

Lance and Billy Bob step away from the group. Billy Bob grabs a spruce log and tosses it into the pit. "L, live by your wits!" he whispers to Lance. "Animals are scared of fire."

"Right behind you, my brother, right behind you," Lance says and tosses in another log.

The students join Lance and Billy Bob around the fire pit. Their chant fades as they stare into the growing flames.

## Chapter 18

# NOW THAT WE'RE ALONE –
# HOO-AH!

Jeffrey sits admiring the blazing fire, chewing on flamed rabbit, and listening to the chorus of wailing loons and coyotes in the distance. *Makes the night eerily beautiful,* he notes. Though Lance and Billy Bob sit a little apart sneaking a beer, and Jonathan is off taking a leak, he assumes, Jeffrey notices how the rest of the students are coupled around the campfire, chewing on their rabbit, sipping their water, shoulder to shoulder, knee to knee, keeping warm in unity. *Unity ... yeah*, he feels strangely at one with the group, he's surprised to realize. *Maybe it's the night. The wilderness. The fire.* Jeffrey turns to Doris sitting next to him and sees that her eyes glisten, mesmerized by the snap and pop of the jumping flames. He observes the group more closely. They, too, seem entranced by the blaze. They touch one another—perhaps unwittingly: a rub of the inner thigh here, a hand down a back there. Doris's leg grazes his ... and it feels quite calming. *Maybe O'Sullivan is right. Maybe this weekend will change me ... us.* He tosses his gnawed rabbit bones into the pit, and watches them sear. *I'm so dehydrated*, he thinks, and reaches for his canteen. Patting nothing but dirt, he gropes the ground. *Where did it go?* He starts to rise, but Doris presses down on his leg.

"Where are you going?" she whispers.

"I think I left my canteen in the tent," he tells her.

She takes a swig from hers and leans in close. "Here," she purrs, "we can share mine."

Jeffrey focuses on her wet lips as they stretch into an enchanting smile. He licks his own. *I'm bewitched*, he thinks. He takes her canteen, and brings it to his mouth.

"Awooooo!" Zack howls.

Jeffrey nudges Doris. "Look at Zack, thinks he's a coyote."

"I think it's called method acting." Doris giggles.

"Awoooooooo!" Zack tries again.

The coyotes and loons echo.

"Awoooooooo!" Zack belts even louder.

Jeffrey catches Dawn staring fixedly at something above him. *What is she looking at?* He glances over his shoulder.

"Aaaah!" Jonathan caps off behind him, stepping out of the darkness.

*What the fuck?* Jeffrey glares at him, thinking, *Now? He wants to start with me now?*

"Awoooooooo!" Zack goes on.

"Aaaah!" Jonathan responds with a smile as he casually goes over to take a seat next to Sharon.

Zack howls again, "Awooooo!"

"Aaaah!" Jonathan slides his arm around Sharon and shoots Scott a wink.

Sharon leans into Jonathan.

"Awooooo!" Zack continues.

"Aaaah!" Scott nods, smiling at Jonathan. "Hoo-ah!" Scott belts, changing the beat.

"Hoo-ah!" Jonathan chimes in.

George joins, "Hoo-ah!"

167

Jonathan and his gang take over the chant with a succession of army Hoo-ahs; Jeffrey hates to admit it, but he is amused. *I guess he doesn't want to start … yet,* he thinks.

Rosa, Heather, Abigail and Kimberly join using a softer, funkier tone, transforming the chant into a pop rock chorus. "Hooooo-ah! Hooooo-ah! Hooo-aaaah!" They jump to their feet and start wriggling with total abandon. Rosa swings over to George and begins to grind against him. George runs his hands up her legs and slithers to a stand. "Hooooo-ah! Hooooo-ah! Hooo-aaaah!" Heather moves in and lures Ronald to his feet. The couples' grinding stirs Abigail and she reaches for Zack. "Hooooo-ah! Hooooo-ah! Hooo-aaaah!" Kimberly takes Zack's other hand and they sandwich into him. *What the hey*? Jeffrey thinks, cracking a smile.

Jeffrey turns to Doris and catches Scott staring lusty-eyed at her as she sits, swaying to the rhythm. *Fucking asshole,* Jeffrey digs his fingernails into the spongy moss. Cindy springs up, and wiggles and chants her way over to Scott. She takes his hands, glides them up her body, drawing him to his feet. Jeffrey screws up his face and feels his glasses slide down his nose. As he pushes them back up again, he spots Lance and Billy Bob, who remain seated, swilling beer, and seem as amused as he is by the spectacle. Jonathan stands and pulls Sharon in tight. Jeffrey almost bursts out laughing at the expression of discomfort on Billy Bob's face when his sister begins to rub her pelvis against Jonathan's leg. Jeffrey then sees Lance steer Billy Bob's attention to Dawn, who sits alone, scintillating eyes fixed on Zack, who is ogling Abigail and Kimberly as they grind against each other now.

Zack suddenly begins to wave his arms, and places a finger over his lips. "Shhhh!" he hisses.

*Ha! Looks like the movie star's feeling abandoned,* Jeffrey laughs to himself, *time for one of his monologues, I bet.*

Zack continues to hiss until he has everyone's attention and, one by one, the students take a seat around the fire once more. The night becomes deathly quiet, save for the sound of burning wood and noisy crickets. Even the distant howls have faded to nothing, Jeffrey notices.

"It's show time, folks!" Lance announces.

Zack stretches his arms theatrically and begins, "Legend has it, that many, many years ago, here in these mountains, during a full moon, a couple came camping and were doing the dirty in a tent like this," he points at his tent. "And due to her moaning and groaning, they couldn't hear the sound of the zipper going up. And as she was on

169

top—and wriggling like a snake—he couldn't see the shadow of the beast as it reached in," he gestures, "grabbed her by her funbags and dragged her into the woods." He pauses, passing his eyes over all of them. "But luckily for the guy, he was celebrating a promotion which included a silver pen or something … I can't remember what it was to be exact … but he took that silver thing and, naked and all, jumped on top of the werewolf and stabbed it numerous times as it was giving his woman the crank of her life while she stared into the fugliest eyes she'd ever orgasmed to." He takes a deep breath.

Jeffrey is impressed. *Not bad, not bad,* he thinks, *he's got them all on the edge of their seats.*

"But before killing it," Zack continues. "… it bit him … and his wife … and apparently … planted its demon seed inside her. They say," he adds in a raspy voice, "the three of them are still lurking out here. Killing. At every full moon."

They all glance up: the impressive, round moon glares down on them. The wind whistles, sending shivers down Jeffrey's back. Zack belts out a long, loud howl.

"Get the fuck out of here!" Scott and Jonathan blurt out.

"That's from a movie, *pendejo*," George says.

"Had you going, didn't I?" Zack says, laughing.

The boys toss pebbles and twigs at Zack, jeering.

*Idiots*, Jeffrey thinks. "Actually, it's from three different werewolf films," he tells them.

"Four," Doris corrects him. "*The Curse of the Werewolf, Big Bad Wolf, Bad Moon* and—"

"*Soldier Dogs*," Zack interrupts.

"*Dog Soldiers*!" Jeffrey says, and notices Billy Bob and Lance gawking at him. *What, I can't be part of the conversation?* he wants to tell them.

"Yeah, yeah, I saw that," George says. "Pretty scary shit but ... I didn't buy the werewolves."

"Yeah, they didn't look real," Zack agrees.

"And what are real werewolves supposed to look like?" Doris asks, grabbing her canteen from Jeffrey. "If it's fiction, then you can make a werewolf look like anything, no?" She takes a swig.

All eyes are on Doris, Jeffrey sees. *You tell them, baby, you tell them.*

"So you think werewolves are fiction?" Zack asks her.

"Fuck no, man, I didn't say that." She tosses her canteen to Jeffrey.

171

"Whoa, whoa, take it easy, Wolf Girl." Zack throws his hands in the air. "Don't get your thong in a knot."

Everyone—but Dawn, Jeffrey notices—laughs, especially Jonathan, who gives Zack the thumbs up.

Jeffrey takes a swig and sees that Doris is digging her barbed bracelets into the back of her head. He scowls at Zack and a sudden rush of heat spreads through Jeffrey's body. *You too? I'll fix you, asshole.*

Doris smacks her hands against her thighs and sits up straight. "All I said," she states, "is that when you're making a movie and have never had the chance to see a *real* werewolf, all you have is your imagination ... or whatever you learned from watching other werewolf films." She grabs her canteen. "So you can't knock someone's film because you think that the werewolves didn't look real, especially if you've never seen one. Maybe those filmmakers saw a real werewolf and that's what it looks like." She takes a long swig.

Jeffrey has never seen Doris so spunky. He feels his heart swell.

"There's no such thing as werewolves," Lance cuts in. "Just a bunch of shit made up to scare people,"

"How do you know that for sure?" Zack asks, and pitches a stone into the fire.

"'Cause I do," Lance spits back.

Zack stands. "What if I told you that one of us *is* a werewolf?" He gazes at all of them. "Hmm?"

They eye him, frowning, open-mouthed. Jeffrey can feel his arms prickle.

"I wouldn't believe it," Lance says, and pulls up his jacket collar.

"Neither would I," Billy Bob concurs, rubbing his knuckles.

Zack takes a step toward Lance. "Let's just say that one of us *is*," he says, "for real," and then continues, in a low whisper. "Would you be able to sleep tonight?"

They all eye one another, wary, and many glances stop on Jeffrey and Doris.

*Yeah, I wish*, Jeffrey thinks.

"What are you talking about? Who, motherfucker?" Lance scans the group. "Who?"

Leaves rustle and a chill creeps down Jeffrey's spine. He squints and looks across the fire. Jonathan has his arms wrapped around his knees and is looking over his shoulder. *Hmm*, Jeffrey thinks, *Zack may be an asshole but he sure knows how to tell a great campfire story. Even Jerkoff Johnson's creeped out.*

173

"You see? You're starting to react," Zack tells them. "It's that simple. It's like we all see each other as 'normal', but as soon as we grow suspicious of someone, we get paranoid and start to create the illusion that they're a monster." He snaps a twig. "But is it an illusion?"

Lance slaps his thigh. "What the fuck are you saying, Hollywood?" he demands.

"Okay, I'll make it easier," Zack says, "How many of you girls would spread 'em for Rob Pattinson?"

Rosa, Heather, Abigail and Kimberly shoot their arms in the air, spread their legs, and pant. *Okay ...*, Jeffrey thinks.

"All of you. Now, imagine you're in a dark alley and a raging Rob Pattinson comes out of nowhere, grabs you, throws you to the ground and takes what you would otherwise give him gladly. Would you see a gorgeous Robert Pattinson, or a monster?" –*Zack is on fire once again*, Jeffrey notes, *he's got them in the palm of his hand*— "What is a monster?" Zack asks the group. "Something that grows hair all over and howls? Could be. But the real monster is within, and when it comes out, it's as fugly as you see it, or as it *lets* you see it." He turns to Doris and Jeffrey, "And to answer Doris

174

about me not liking the werewolves in *Soldier Dogs*—"

"*Dog Soldiers*!" Doris and Jeffrey blurt out.

"Right," Zack apologizes, holding up his hands. "I guess they just didn't scare me. Then again, I don't scare easy." He winks at Abigail and Kimberly.

Scott quacks like a duck and everyone cracks up.

"Well, I'd do Rob Pattinson even at his fugliest," Kimberly declares.

"Hoo-ah!" Rosa, Heather, and Abigail shout.

Jeffrey glances at Doris, wondering if she would do Rob Pattison too. He shakes off the ugly thought.

The sounds of howling coyotes and loons start up again. Jeffrey notices Billy Bob and Lance jerk back. *Ha! They're scared of the howls*, Jeffrey laughs to himself.

"Yeah, some girls are sick enough to go for that," Zack says.

"I'll bet you Doris here would spread 'em for a werewolf. Wouldn't you, Wolf Girl?" Ronald teases.

"I'll be your werewolf, Doris," Scott croons, and howls like a wolf.

Jeffrey turns to Doris, ready to defend—*Is she smiling?* Jeffrey feels his neck tighten and bares his teeth. He notices Cindy squirm on her log. Her hand is resting on Scott's thigh. She grabs his crotch. And squeezes hard. *Good!* Jeffrey thinks.

"Ouch! Bitch!" Scott yells, and whips her hand off.

"No," Cindy jumps in front of Scott and points, "*You*! Bitch!" She takes a swing at his face but he blocks it. She kicks a blazing branch at him but he boots it back into the pit.

"You fucking prick!" she screams, and storms off.

Scott brushes the embers off his pants. "Oww! Fuck!" He licks his scorched fingers. "Kitty!" he hollers after Cindy. "Kitty!" He laughs. "Here, kitty, kitty, kitty," he calls out into the forest.

Jeffrey glances over at Scott, who is smiling at Doris. Jeffrey turns Doris around to face him. "Are you smiling at him?" he hisses.

"What?" she says.

"Were you flirting him?" Jeffrey interrogates, frowning.

"What are you talking about?" she says, and reaches for her canteen.

"Nothing," he says, and spins on his log. His boot hits metal. He reaches down, picks up the

176

canteen, and is about to take a swig. *Wait a second,* he thinks. He turns to Doris: she drinks from her canteen. He examines the one in his hand. *How the hell didn't I see my canteen before?* He shifts his eyes to the ground, then back to Doris, and shakes his head. *Fucking girl's got me losing my mind.* He takes a swig.

Sharon gets to her feet. "You shouldn't have said that," she tells Scott.

"Said what?" he raises his shoulders.

Sharon points at Doris, "That thing about being her werewolf. It was rude!" she marches off into the woods.

Scott yells out, "Why don't you mind—"

"She's right, dude," Billy Bob interjects. "You don't even have a moustache."

"At least her boyfriend here has sideburns," Jonathan needles.

Jeffrey turns to Jonathan. *Yeah, that's right, go ahead, laugh … you'll see.*

"Nah, he's no wolfman," Zack cuts in. "Only one hairy enough to be a werewolf among us isn't among us."

"Damn! That one-eyebrowed sand dog does look like a werewolf," Ronald says. "Ever see him in the showers? He's covered with fur, wall to wall."

"Is he a wolf down there?" Abigail asks, and points at Ronald's groin.

"The fuck I'd know?" he blurts.

"You know what they say about hairy men?" Kimberly says.

"Great in bed!" Rosa, Heather, Abigail, and Kimberly shout in unison.

*What a bunch of cockteasers*, Jeffrey thinks.

"Yeah, if he's such a big bad wolf," Scott says, "then why isn't he here with us?" He winks at his buddies.

*I wonder what that means*, Jeffrey thinks. *What did they do to him?*

"He's probably too busy with his Russian hottie," George answers, "I know I'd be."

"You would, would you?" Rosa puts both hands on her hips and raises her brows.

*Oh, oh!* Jeffrey thinks. *Dummy just put his foot in his mouth.*

"I mean with you, *mami*," George catches himself.

"Maybe he's more man than all of you," Rosa says. "To want to spend a weekend with his girl … alone. Hey, some men are lovers, some are …" she gestures male masturbation, stands, and bats her eyelashes at George. "Which are you, *papi*?" She

178

turns on her heels, wiggles her curvy hips and heads for her tent.

George jumps to his feet, howls, and follows.

Jeffrey glances at Doris.

"I know who's getting some tonight," Scott says.

*Me. I hope*, Jeffrey thinks.

"Not you, that's for sure," Lance ribs Scott.

"Right …" Scott says with a huge grin, eyes glued on Doris.

Heather whispers into Ronald's ear and heads for her tent.

Ronald, open-mouthed, springs up and follows after her.

The boys hoot and cheer.

Lance pats his pockets. "Shit, I forgot to bring my earplugs!"

Ronald gives them the thumbs up then flips them the finger.

Zack gets up. "Be back in a sec," he tells Abigail and Kimberly, and disappears into his tent.

Jeffrey catches Scott blowing Doris a kiss. She stands—not taking her eyes off Scott. "I'm outta here, too," she says flatly, and heads for her tent.

*What the fuck was that all about?* Jeffrey shoots Scott a look. Sparkling green eyes. Strong jaw. Broad shoulders. Jeffrey is jealous.

Scott grins, "Welly, welly, welly. Beauty and the freak," he points at Jeffrey. "I think your girl's got the hots for me."

Jeffrey takes a swig from his canteen.

"Cheers, partner!" Scotts says, and holds up his water bottle.

Silently boiling, Jeffrey stands, brushes the dirt off his pants and heads for Doris's tent.

"Save some for me, pard!" Scott shouts out to him.

*\*\**

"Yup," Scott continues, "that chick's got a hard on for me."

"Eh? What?" Jonathan says, peering over his shoulder at the tall, shadowed pines that stretch up like arrows into the cloudless sky.

"I said that that chick-"

"Do you hear that?" Jonathan exclaims, his back to Scott.

"What?"

"That hum."

"You guys coming?" Lance says.

Jonathan jerks around and finds Lance and Billy Bob standing over them. Lance raises his eyebrows and mimics smoking a joint.

"No, I'm good," Jonathan tells him and takes a swig of water, looking over his shoulder again.

"Me, too," Scott says, eyes on Doris's tent. "Catch you guys later."

Lance and Billy Bob throw their hands up at one another, and go off into the woods. They cross Zack, who returns with his sleeping bag. He spreads it in front of the campfire and invites Abigail and Kimberly to join him.

Dawn, gaping at Zack, stuffs her earphones into her ears, turns up the music, and creeps off.

Sharon hurries over, "I can't find Cindy." She glances about then tells Scott, "I think you should go look for her."

"Fuck her," he says dismissively. "You go."

"I just did!" Sharon looks to Jonathan, but he seems focused on something behind him. She glares at Scott and stomps off.

A screech owl's piercing shriek cuts into the night. Zack and the girls screech back.

"*Cállate, coño!*" Rosa cackles from inside her tent.

\*\*\*

The owl screeches again. Doris sits on her knees guzzling water from her canteen. "I'm fucking thirsty as hell," she says. "Must be the air up here. It's dry." She unrolls the tent's musty fabric window and Velcros it shut.

"I'm talking to you!" Jeffrey snaps. "What's up with you and that fucking Scott?"

"I didn't smile at him!" she says, and rolls out her sleeping bag. "What's wrong with you?"

"I saw what I saw," he says, and crosses his arms over his chest.

"Exactly," she says, spreading her hands across her bag, smoothing the wrinkles.

He points a finger at her. "You just remember that last night they all pissed in your face."

"That, I will never fucking forget."—She pulls off her knit hat—"Don't worry about me,"—She ruffles her hair—"everything is hunky-Doris,"— She starts to unzip her coat—"so stop imagining things."

"I just need to know you're with me!" he says in a loud whisper, and then pulls a gun out from under his pants.

She digs into her coat pocket. "I am," she says, and takes out a matching gun. "So now fuckin' kiss me." She pulls off his glasses and moves in.

\*\*\*

"There it is again." Jonathan continues to examine the trees. "Don't you hear it?" he asks Scott.

"What? Another motorbike?" Scott sneers, eyes still on Doris's tent.

"No …" Jonathan scans the treetops. "Listen."

182

The screech owl shrieks.

"Fucking owl sounds like Cindy having a fit." Scott chuckles.

"No, something else ... something ... *mechanical ... robotic ...*," Jonathan says, "coming from up there." He points at the treetops.

"We're way away from any robots up here, dude," he says, "I think the altitude is making you hear shit."

Jonathan gets up. "Well, I'm going to go check it out."

"Yeah, all right," Scott says. "You do that." He watches his friend disappear into the dense woods, and considers the thick, erect cedars. He places a hand on his crotch and turns his attention back to Doris's tent.

\*\*\*

Doris and Jeffrey kiss savagely. Hands pawing each other's bodies, they are ravenous for flesh, for love, for air. They pull apart, panting like dogs, gasping for breath.

The owl shrieks again.

"Let me get some water," Doris says, and reaches for her canteen.

"Me too," Jeffrey says, and reaches for his.

They drink voraciously.

"Shit, I'm all out," she says after a moment, and tosses her canteen to the side. Jeffrey guzzles his water: she's riveted, and licks her lips with every gulp he takes. Her hand shoots forth, "Save some for me!" She grabs his canteen as he's drinking; water splashes his face. "Sorry." She gives him an impish smile, reaches over, wipes the water off his mouth and licks her fingers. "Mind if I have some?" she asks, and drinks before he can answer.

Jeffrey watches, goggle-eyed, as she takes a long swig. "That's enough," he yanks the canister away from her, screws the cap back on and drops it out of Doris's reach. All without taking his eyes off her. He pulls her in close and savors her neck, her chin, her mouth. His fingers search and find her pant button. He struggles with it and finally pops it open.

"Wait," she says, pushing him off, "I need to pee." She reaches for her coat.

"Fuck!" Jeffrey blurts out, and pounces forward, groping her as she puts on her jacket. He presses himself hard against her as she unzips the tent.

"I *really* need to pee!" Doris begs.

Jeffrey gets a firm hold of her hair and brings her ear to his mouth when, from the tent's open flap, something catches his eye. He quickly reaches for and puts on his glasses. "Me, too, I need to pee," Jeffrey says, with an icy glare, as he watches Jonathan standing alone in the distance, looking up at the trees.

Doris zips up her coat. "Be right back." She grabs his chin and kisses him, biting him hard.

"Oww!" Jeffrey touches his lip, tasting metal.

She licks the blood off his mouth. "Pussy," she says, and crawls out.

Again, the owl screeches.

Jeffrey grabs Doris by her boot. "Hey, watch your ass out there."

"You watch it from in there." She wiggles her behind.

"I'm not kidding," he says, "You just be ready … for anything."

"Don't worry about me—" Doris pats her right pocket "—*you* be ready," she says, and exits.

Eyes on Jonathan, Jeffrey downs what's left in his canteen.

The owl shrieks again. An expert would note the mechanical tone. And, from the same treetop, a camera lens zooms in.

Chapter 19

# WE ALL GOT SHIT

"So?" Brian asks.

Tim O'Sullivan beams. He studies his younger brother, who now—more than ever—reminds him of their father. Cleft chin. Dark blue beady eyes set against almost jet-black hair. Handsome, chiseled face. Darwin-esque large forehead and receding hairline. He tries, Tim knows, yet even with the Fremont gray-plaid flannel shirt, the Calvin Klein black puffer vest, and straight-leg Armani jeans,

Brian O'Sullivan can't shake off his lab geek aura. His genius.

Brian hits a button on a keyboard and the sound of the screeching owl stops. He lifts an eyebrow. "What do you think, Tim?"

Both men turn to the four computer monitors on the long wooden dining table. The screens—in night vision mode—reveal several campers: a close up of Jeffrey stepping out of Doris's tent; Doris marching into the woods; Zack, Kimberly and Abigail lounging on a sleeping bag by the campfire; Lance and Billy Bob standing near a tree.

"It's ... great ...." The older O'Sullivan is beside himself. He paces the log cabin's worn oak floor. "I mean ... Jeffrey Dalton and Doris Mitchell assertive, in a conversation with Jonathan Johnson and the others ... all of them, unafraid. Howling along, screeching back, walking into the dark. I didn't think it would happen so fast."

"If you think four years of development is fast, I salute you," Brian snorts.

"They're adapting incredibly," O'Sullivan says, spying Jeffrey head into the forest.

"Just as I promised," Brian boasts, and raises his coffee cup to his lips.

"Is everything else as planned?" O'Sullivan asks, eyes glued on the monitors.

187

"Yup, and you can thank my fiancée for that," Brian says with a smile, glancing at the stairs that lead to the bedrooms.

O'Sullivan turns to him. "Yeah, congratulations on that," he offers, flatly.

Brian's right cheek begins to spasm—a tic he developed when his brother accidently hit him with a baseball in the face during Little League practice. "What is it, Tim?"

"Nothing." O'Sullivan averts his eyes to the hunting rifle mounted on a rack above the fireplace, the ledge stone hearth beneath, and focuses his gaze on the subdued flames. "Fire needs more stoking." He moves toward the small firewood bin. "Bin's empty," he says, picking it up. "I'll go—"

"No, come on," Brian crosses the modest living room behind his brother. "Spit it out."

"I, ah ..." O'Sullivan opens the back door and reaches for a log from the neat pile—wide enough to last the winter—stacked against the stone wall. "I just think six months is too soon, that's all," he admits. He fills the bin, and bends to lift it, but stops when his leg shoots a pain straight through to his foot. "How well do you know her?"

Brian laughs, "You've never been in love, Tim. Love has no time. It sneaks up on you." He takes

188

the bin from his brother and hauls it across the room.

"Right ... but ..." O'Sullivan glimpses the stairs leading to the provisional laboratory they've set up in the basement. "Should she really *be* here?"

"Ahh! *That's* the question." Brian smiles, and sets down the bin. "Hey, I needed help, and with you at the school full time, there was no one else I could trust." He tosses a log into the fireplace. "And," he throws his brother a wink, "it gets lonely up here."

"Right," O'Sullivan says, sourly. He hobbles over and sips his cold coffee.

Brian pats his arm, "Everything is going to be A-okay. And wait 'til you see what we have in store for them." Brian hits keys and the screens switch to different areas of the woods.

"I can't see it," O'Sullivan says, squinting, and steps closer.

"Hang on a sec, let me zoom in." Brian clicks a command. "No ... no ... too hidden ... you'll have to wait 'til morning." He switches back to the campground cameras. "But don't worry, nothing too dangerous. Just enough to keep them on their toes," Brian grins, "or *off*."

"They'll be fine," O'Sullivan says.

Skimming a list of names with photos on the table, Brain looks up at his brother after a moment. "You said there were eighteen, where are the other two?" he asks.

"Elie El-Hage and Alex Peterson. They'll be here," the older brother assures.

*** 

Dilly ambles down the stairs and stops at the bottom to check herself in the mirror by the front door. Her leather pants are creased and her leather jacket is zipped down enough to reveal her bra. *Damn, I'm hot*, she thinks. She runs her fingers through her disheveled brown hair, and yawns herself awake. "Babe, I'm hungry," she moans, sashaying over to the living room. "Oh … hey, Tim." She zips up her jacket.

"Did you have fun with my kids?" O'Sullivan chaffs.

"Horny little fuckers," she comments, and kisses the top of Brian's head, taking in his scent of Acqua Di Gio. "Someone ought to spank 'em." She turns to warm her hands by the hissing fire.

"Yeah, well, they've been there and they've been done that," O'Sullivan says, "That's their problem."

A monitor reveals Zack kissing Abigail while Kimberly caresses Abigail's hair.

"They're teens," Dilly says, heading to the open kitchen, "what kind of problems can they have besides wanting to get laid?"

"Are they teens?" O'Sullivan asks. "I don't think they've ever even been given half the chance to be kids."

*Shit, no coffee*, Dilly sees, and pours out the pot's grainy remains. "You guys want more coffee?" She opens a creaky cupboard and notices dusty soup cans tucked in the far corner, a yellowing box of crackers, and grime. "The scraps of three generations," she grumbles, and pulls out the jar of ground Arabica beans she picked up in town.

"Yes, please," Brian answers. "Coffee."

Dilly turns the coffeemaker on before she joins him at the monitors. Together they scan O'Sullivan's list. Brian points to a girl on the screen. "Who's she?" he asks.

Dilly's studied the profiles—she can match names to faces quite well; even though they're all tinted green now. She's about to answer, but Tim cuts her off.

"Abigail Simmons," he answers, "maladaptive perfectionist. Mother, Major Louise Simmons, killed in Iraq." On screen, Zack finds Kimberly's mouth; Abigail bites the back of his

191

neck. O'Sullivan points, "Kimberly Jones, bipolar disorder. Father, EOD team leader, Bradley Jones, spattered somewhere in Kabul." Zack goes from one mouth to the other. "Zack Schwartz," O'Sullivan continues, "narcissistic personality disorder. Father, special ops commander, David Schwartz, alive and kicking ... kicking the shit out of his son every chance he gets."

They turn to Monitor 3, and Dilly leans in closer. On the wide shot, two students stand along the perimeter, their backs to the camera. Brian switches views but trees block each angle. "Who's that?" he asks.

"Billy Bob Jenkins and Lance Willis," O'Sullivan responds.

The boys step into the camera's view. "Watch this," Billy Bob tells Lance, and front-kicks the tree.

"The twin and the football star we read about who saved his mother and little brother," Dilly says, proud of her research.

O'Sullivan points at Lance, who is guffawing at Billy Bob—his boot cleat is stuck in the tree. "Lance Willis," O'Sullivan says, "only one in the program who doesn't need to be in the program. Only one with no military background. Just the street ... a natural survivor." Billy Bob tugs at his boot with two hands. Lance splits his sides, laughing. "Fearless. That's why I had to have him." O'Sullivan taps the screen. "Willis took out a vicious hoodlum at fourteen years old to save his kin. And look at him, well adapted and bright." They watch Billy Bob look to his friend for help. Lance frees Billy Bob's boot with ease. "And strong. I can already see him leading his own platoon."

"Big boy," Dilly says. "But why the twin?" She asks, pointing at Billy Bob. "He's tiny like his sister. Seems weak. What's he good for?"

Billy Bob high-fives Lance. "That one ... he's agile and fast, can improvise and get himself into and out of any kind of mess." O'Sullivan smirks.

"Why his sister?" Brian asks.

"I couldn't, and wouldn't, have one without the other," O'Sullivan answers. "They're special. Sharon and he can feel each other. I'm curious to see what they'd be like in a combat situation."

***

Billy Bob and Lance sit up against a tree along the clearing's periphery, smoking a monster joint and swilling beer.

Lance sniffs the pungent aroma. "Where'd you get this shit, my brother?" he asks, and passes the joint. "I'm seeing things."

Billy Bob takes the spliff. "It's the same shit we always smoke," he says, and inhales deeply.

193

Lance points over the tents and across the fire pit, "Then why am I seeing Hollywood having a … threesome."

"No shit." Billy Bob says, stretching up his neck. "Is that Dawn creepin' for a peepin'?" He chuckles.

"Looks like she's coming back from the dead," Lance chortles. "What's with that chick?" He slips his hand under his toque to scratch the day old stubble on his head.

Billy Bob raises his brows, "You don't know?" he asks, and offers the joint.

"No, lay it on me, my brother." Lance takes a long toke and holds in the smoke. "This has got to be good."

Dawn stands on the opposite side of the pit ogling Zack and the girls. "Dawn suffers from posttraumatic stress disorder," Billy Bob murmurs.

"We all got shit." Lance exhales the smoke in an enormous opaque cloud.

Billy Bob takes a swig of beer and begins to explain. "Both her parents do a one year stint in Iraq. They survive the shit and come back, and check this out," he takes the joint from Lance, "they go to her granddad's, who's been taking care of her all this time. Pick her up, and roll towards home sweet home when out of nowhere a drunken fucker trucker hauling oil falls asleep at the wheel and BAM! He totals their car sending Dawn flying into oblivion. But by some fucking fluke—or maybe it just 'wasn't her time'—Dawn gets up with not even a scratch on her and makes her way back to the flaming car. Watched her parents crawl out of it, both lit up like a bonfire."

Lance considers Dawn, who's inching toward the threesome. "Damn ..." he whispers. The campfire's reds and yellows bounce off her pale skin.

"They say Dawn was talking to them as they lay there, burnt to a crisp," Billy Bob continues, "when all of a sudden her mom opens her eyes and reaches out for her ... just before she croaked she zombied Dawn's ass!"

***

"What's spooning?" Dawn asks as she hovers over Zack, Kimberly and Abigail. *Why are they looking at me like that?* she wonders, seeing the surprised looks on their faces.

"Oh my God!" Kimberly squawks, startled.

"It speaks!" Zack says, obviously shocked and amused. "Did you hear her?" he whispers to the girls under his arms. "She spoke! The girl hasn't spoken in five years!"

"And all she wants to know is —" Abigail begins to say.

"What's spooning?" Dawn repeats, standing as still as she is able.

Zack turns to Abigail and Kimberly.

Abigail runs her fingertips over the sleeping bag and winks at Zack. "Show her," she suggests.

"Show her?" Zack says, with a dumbfounded look on his face.

"Yes," Abigail says.

Kimberly pushes Zack down on to his side. "Yeah, show her." Her marble blue eyes shimmer.

"Okay," he says, "since you *both* insist." He smiles up at Dawn and pats the empty space in front of him. "Lie down here, honey."

Dawn pulls off her earphones and sets her iPod on the sleeping bag. A slow bass and snare drum rhythm plays as she reclines, facing him. He gently turns her so she faces out.

"*This* is spooning," Zack tells Dawn and wraps an arm around her. He presses up against her.

Dawn feels him grow. *Is that what I think it is?* she marvels. She rubs against him. Her skin tingles and she feels herself getting wet. She rolls on top of him, pressing her open mouth on his, and slips in her tongue.

196

"That is so sexy," Kimberly whispers.

"*You* are so sexy," Abigail purrs.

Dawn watches Kimberly pull a cocklebur out of Abigail's tousled strawberry blond curls, and is overcome by a series of explosive convulsions when she sees the girls kiss.

***

"Check it, man, check it," Lance says, craning his neck. "Girl fags!"

"Did you hear her, bro?" Billy Bob asks. "She spoke!"

"Yeah, my man," Lance murmurs, eyes fixed on Dawn.

"What did she say?" Bill Bob says.

"Who the fuck cares?" he mumbles. "I'd do her, mute." He spies Dawn bounce up and down on Zack while Kimberly and Abigail kiss and caress him. "Fucking … Hollywood!"

"Wow," Billy Bob utters, "either we are completely whacked or those people are on fucking E." He takes a long toke.

"That is so fucked up," Lance says, grabbing himself.

***

"They're all fucked up," O'Sullivan tells his brother, as they turn away from the screens. "They all have something. They've been through the shit.

197

That's why they all need to be here. To break from their traumas. Turn their fear into bravery. Give them confidence." He lifts his cup, *Shit, it's empty*, and sets it down again.

Brian breathes in the aroma of the beans brewing. "Dilly, how's the coffee coming?"

"Be ready in a minute," she says, moving away from him. "I'm going to toast some bread. You want some?"

Brian jerks his chin at his brother, who shakes his head. "No, we're fine, thanks." He looks back at the screens. "Yeah, it's all about confidence," he agrees.

"It's like your first fistfight," O'Sullivan says. "You're scared."

"I crapped my pants," Brian admits.

"I remember," his brother tells him, "but what about your next fight?"

"Less scared," Brian says. "And that one, I won." He pats himself on the chest.

"It's also like the first time you have sex," Dilly says from the kitchen, as she rummages through the freezer.

"Exactly," O'Sullivan agrees. "You're scared. But once you pass that fear—" He stops himself.

"You can do it over and over again," Dilly finishes. "And enjoy it."

*Like your first kill.* O'Sullivan smiles to himself.

"But will it work this time around?" Brian asks.

"New and improved, no?" O'Sullivan tilts his head.

Brian puts an arm around his big brother. "As long as it's under control."

O'Sullivan nods. "And look," he points at Dawn on the screen. "It's working on Evans, so I know it'll work on all of them." He looks at Brian, feeling the heat radiate through his own chest. "By the end of this weekend, they'll all have the makings to become American fighting machines."

"If only the old man were alive to see," Brian says under his breath.

The coffee machine gurgles the last drops of water. The toaster emits a sweet scent while the bread chars. On the monitor, a chorus of moans and groans emanate from Zack and the girls as well as Rosa and Heather's tents.

"Are you guys watching porn?" Dilly asks from the kitchen. She pops a breakfast burrito into the microwave. Presses the start button. The power in the cabin goes out.

***

"I'm telling you," Billy Bob says, indicating a clump of shrubs in the thick forest, "something moved behind those bushes."

"Probably someone doing the two," Lance tells him. He takes a drag from the joint and passes it back.

"You think?" Billy Bob says, still glancing all around.

"With all that water?"

Billy Bob takes a toke. "Shit!"

"You know," Lance says.

A gust of wind slips through the trees. Billy Bob starts.

"What are you, paranoid?" Lance says. "Give me that." He takes the spliff.

"Scott said J.J. thinks the A-rab's up here," Billy Bob says. "He said he heard his bike." He picks up a twig and fondles it nervously.

"There's no way …" Lance takes another hit.

"How do you know?" Billy Bob retorts, snapping the twig into tiny pieces. "You said he said he was going to kill you guys."

"Well, he doesn't know it was us …" Lance scratches the back of his neck, "for *sure*." He finds a squished earwig on his fingertips and wipes it on his pants.

200

A limb from a nearby tree crashes to the ground. Billy Bob whips around. It rolls toward them. "Look, look, look!" He nudges Lance's shoulder, knocking the joint out of his hand.

"The fuck!" Lance feels the ground for the doobie as he scans the trees. "Shit! Now you got *me* all paranoid! Ouch!" The ember stings his fingertips. He takes a last drag and flicks the roach. "Let's go find J.J."

Chapter 20

# THE BIG BAD WOLVES

Jonathan scans the trees with his flashlight. The buzzing. The robotic hums. Surely he's not hearing things. The ground comes to an abrupt end; the edge of a hill, he realizes. *Good place to take a piss*, he thinks. He unzips and listens to the drizzling stream. The sound gives him an idea of the hill's slope. *Do survival books give this valuable tip? Ha!* He laughs to himself. A crack sounds from somewhere in the dark. He shines his flashlight into the treetops and works his way to the ground.

Nothing. *Light must have scared it off,* he figures. But the sound of his stream gets drowned by the clamor of marching feet. He looks to his right and finds Jeffrey standing next to him. Unfazed, Jonathan continues to urinate. "What do you want?" he barks.

Jeffrey eyeballs him as he reaches under his coat and unzips his pants.

"Oh, you want some of this, don't you?" Jonathan shakes himself dry and zips up his pants. "Sorry geek, I'm not a—"

"I know what he's doing to you," Jeffrey says. "O'Sullivan. I saw when I was in detention."

"I don't know what you *think* you—" Jonathan stops, feeling warmth on his leg. "What the fuck?"

Jeffrey is peeing on him. He juts out his chin and smirks.

Jonathan throws a punch that Jeffrey catches like it's nothing but air.

\*\*\*

Doris sees everything. "Jeffrey!" she cries under her breath, and leaps out from behind the shrubs. She goes for her right pocket but a hand covers her mouth and pulls her back in.

"Little Red Riding Hood, Little Red Riding Hood," Scott whispers into her ear, "I'm gonna—"

"Fuck you!" Jonathan yells and punches Jeffrey in the stomach with his free fist. Jonathan belts out a painful yowl on impact, jerking his hand.

In one swift motion, Jeffrey pulls out the gun tucked under his belt.

"Whoa! Whoa! Whoa!" Jonathan shoots up his arms. "Take it easy! What the … you … you … you wouldn't. Come on, man," Jonathan begs. "What did I do?"

Jeffrey screws up his face and cocks the hammer.

"No! No!" Jonathan cries out.

"Hey, J.J.," Billy Bob calls as he and Lance stumble into the scene.

Jeffrey whips around and aims his gun at them.

Lance jumps back. "What the-"

Jonathan leaps at Jeffrey, dropkicking him from behind. The brain-rattling blow to the head sends his wire-rimmed glasses flying. Jeffrey jerks sideways and loses his grip on the gun. He clearly watches it soar as he stumbles and is aghast at the sight of his enemy leaping for his weapon.

"Get him!" Jonathan yells, clamping a trembling hand on to the gun.

Jeffrey gets to his feet and dives for Jonathan but is tackled mid-air by Lance. The humongous Tight End's bone-jarring blow sends Jeffrey tumbling down the slope.

*** 

Scott holds his privates, moaning in pain, as Doris tries to claw her way out of the bushes. "Where do you think you're going?" he grunts, seizing her left leg. He drags her back toward him, digs his powerful fingers into her left shoulder and flips her on to her back. Doris flails her arms, landing a few slaps, but Scott easily pins her arms over her head with one forearm as he throws his weight on top of her. Doris's head thrashes about and she bites repeatedly into the air, grunting, screaming. He digs his chin into her right cheek and kisses and licks her ear. "What the fuck?" he growls, grabbing her breasts hard. "What do you got on?"

Doris tries to squirm out from under him but Scott presses against her even harder. "I told you. I want that sexy fuckin' ass," he says through gritted teeth, ripping her pants button. He forces her over onto her stomach and viciously tries to yank her pants down.

"No! No!" Doris screams. "Not again! Not again!" She tears a hand free and swings her barbed wrist into Scott's face—stabbing skin,

205

nearly cutting into eye—and knocks him to the side.

"Fucking bitch!" he snarls.

She digs into her coat pocket, clutches her gun, and points it at his face.

"Holy fucking shit!" Scott bellows in one breath, and his years of MMA training are revealed with a breakneck slap to her hand that sends the weapon flying. He pounces on top of her again, roaring as his limbs envelop her.

A high-pitched shriek cuts the night. Scott lifts his eyes: Cindy darts, screaming, towards him holding a rock the size of a football over her head. He rolls to the side as she brings it down and it lands on Doris's skull, knocking her unconscious.

A thunderous growl resonates through the forest.

Cindy wails as she flies into the opposite trees.

Scott snatches Doris's gun and springs to his feet. "Cindy!" he calls after her.

"What the fuck's goin' on, man?" Jonathan hollers, as he runs toward Scott, pointing Jeffrey's gun into the trees.

Billy Bob and Lance stumble over. Pupils dilated. Bloodshot.

"What the hell was that noise?" Zack echoes from the campsite.

Billy Bob waves his flashlight. "Over here!" he blurts.

***

"Who screamed?" Rosa asks Zack, as she and George scramble out of their tent.

"Sounded like Cindy," Heather says, as she and Ronald emerge from their pop-up.

"Where is she?" Abigail asks, buttoning her pants.

Zack points at the light beam, and hollers, "There!"

***

Scott is on the ground next to a half-conscious Cindy. "Kitty! Kitty!" he shakes her gently.

"Owww," she groans, rubbing her head and slowly returning to consciousness. "I think … the tree … hit my head," she says groggily, pulling off her ponytails. Then, she opens her eyes wide. "You bastard!" she shrieks, and tears at Scott's face.

"I didn't do anything! I didn't do anything!" He tries to block her. "I went to pee and she came at me with a gun!" He catches her hands and softens his voice, "Look what she did to my face."

Cindy winces and bites her lip.

"I was only trying to take the gun away from her, Kitty." Scott snivels.

Cindy caresses his wound, goes limp and leans into his chest, whimpering. He wraps his arms around her.

The gang arrives, each one panting for air.

"Who? What gun?" Zack asks.

"What happened?" Rosa asks.

Kimberly spots Cindy on the ground and rushes toward her. "Cindy!"

"Who has a gun?" George yells.

Billy Bob and Lance are dumbstruck.

"They do!" Heather points at Scott and Jonathan.

Ronald approaches them. "What's going on?" he asks. "Why do you guys have guns?"

"We took them from the geeks!" Jonathan answers.

"What would they be doing with guns?" Zack says.

"What do you think?" Jonathan says, waving the weapon at all of them. "They came here to Columbine our asses!"

The gang gasps almost in unison, taking a step back. A low wind blows. The campfire crackles in the distance.

"What?" Abigail cheeps, holding a hand to her chest.

"Them?" Heather exhales. "Why would they—"

"You're crazy," Rosa tells Jonathan. "The geeks?" She turns to George, "No way!"

Zack walks up to Jonathan. "Why would they want to hurt us?" he asks, brow creased.

"'Cause they're freaks!" Jonathan says, glancing at his boys.

Zack wags his finger. "Maybe *geeks* … but not *freaks*," he declares. "I don't believe it."

"Then why don't we just ask the geeky bitch?" Scott says, tramping over. Everyone follows behind. Scott spins around, and almost bumps into Zack. "She's gone."

"Gone?" Zack repeats.

"She was right there a minute ago," Scott says, pointing at the empty space on the ground. "Where the fuck did she go?" he hollers, waving his gun from side to side.

"Doris?" Zack yells. "Doris?"

Branches break. Pebbles bounce. The group starts.

"It took her," Sharon echoes, pushing past a naked shrub.

"Where you were the fuck?" Billy Bob garbles to his sister, eyes half-lidded.

209

Jonathan steps up to Sharon. "What took her?"

"Whatever hit Cindy," Sharon says somberly.

"What hit you?" Jonathan asks Cindy.

Cindy raises her shoulders, "I don't know."

"Whatever came out from the night," Sharon says, "It growled, hit Cindy, and took Doris."

"What do you mean *it*?" Jonathan asks. "Did you see what *it* was?"

Sharon shakes her head, "It was too dark …."

The wind moans between the knotted trunks.

Scott cocks the gun. "Where's the fucking geek?"

"Over there!" Jonathan sprints, "At the edge of the hill!" he shouts.

Scott and the others tear after Jonathan, trampling through low ferns, and hurtling over fallen trees.

*** 

Scott and Jonathan make their way down, flashing their lights as the others huddle together. They wait at the edge, peering down at the boys.

Scott and Jonathan examine the ground with their lights and come upon a raggedy bundle.

Jonathan kicks at it. A jacket. He picks it up. "Dalton," he says, lighting the nametag sewn over the right breast pocket.

210

The others hold their breath watching the boys make their way back up the hill.

"It's the geek's!" Scott holds up Jeffrey's jacket for all to see: It's mud-spattered. Torn.

"*Dios mio*!" Rosa gasps. "There's blood on the collar!"

"And on the sleeve!" Sharon cries.

"Whatever got *her* got *him*." Scott says, swinging the jacket. Two loaded gun magazines fall with a thud out of Jeffrey's pocket.

\*\*\*

Jonathan picks up the magazines and holds them out. "Whatever got *them* saved *us*," he states. He squeezes the magazines. *Oh my God*, he thinks, *Jeffrey was really going to do it!*

"Thank God," Rosa says.

"Uh-uh," Scott turns to them. "The geeks got got because they were sitting ducks. There's something out there. I say we get it before it gets us."

"Yeah … Yeah!" the group shouts, "Let's get it! Let's get it!" They scour the ground for rocks and branches.

Lance steps forward. "I say we find The Sarge and get the hell out of here!"

"Where?" Scott screams. "Where's the fucking Sarge?"

211

"And how do we know this isn't part of his test?" George offers.

"Yeah! Yeah! How do we know!" some of the others shout.

A motorbike blares in the distance. *The A-Rab!* Jonathan thinks. "It *is* them!" he hollers at Scott. "I knew it!"

"Those fuckers!" Scott charges into the woods. "I'm going to kill them!"

Cindy bolts after him. "Scott!"

Jonathan begins to follow, but Lance cuts in front of him. "We need you here, my brother." He points at Jonathan's gun.

"Who?" Zack asks Jonathan. "*What* fuckers are you talkin' about?"

"Elie …" Billy Bob says, "and his girlfriend."

"Who, Alex?" Sharon asks. "But why?"

"Because they're fucking terrorists," Jonathan yells, "and that's what terrorists do, they fucking terrorize people!"

"Oh, come on," Rosa says. "*En serio?*"

"Alex Peterson," Jonathan continues, "daughter of Ivan Petrov, KGB defector. Works for U.S. Intelligence now? How do we know he's not spying for them?" His arms flail, accenting every word. He feels his own hatred multiply. "And you're going to tell me the A-rab's on *our* side? You

212

people are fuckin' sleeping!" He shakes his fists. "No kidding they're ramming our airplanes through our buildings!"

Chapter 21

# WHO THE HELL ARE YOU, REALLY?

"There!" Brian yells from the basement, as the lights come on.

O'Sullivan paces back and forth side-eyeing Dilly, who is propped on the kitchen counter eating her toast and tapping her bare feet on the cabinet doors as if nothing happened. She holds out a thick emergency candle. "Make a wish," she says, and blows out the flame.

Brian jogs up the stairs. "Now, let's start this baby up and get back on schedule." He returns to the computer.

O'Sullivan continues to eye Dilly; she's gnawing loudly. *Look at that! What does Brian see in her?* Crumbs spill down onto their father's battered oak floors. He can't stop wondering why the fuck his brother even brought her here in the first place. *It's not like we're here for Thanksfuckinggiving dinner.*

"Fuck," Brian says, rubbing his forehead, "It won't start up. Something's wrong with the power supply."

"You're shitting me!" O'Sullivan says, joining his brother.

Brian taps his fingers on the table. "Let me go see if I have another one downstairs." He takes off for the basement.

O'Sullivan glowers at Dilly. *She's crept in like an alley cat*, he thinks, biting his lower lip. "This is your fault, you know that?" he blurts out. "How can you be so stupid? You pushed the microwave start button! Don't you have a microwave at home?"

Dilly fixes her eyes on him.

"Doesn't your power go off when too many things are on at the same time," O'Sullivan barks,

215

"like the coffee machine, toaster, and four fucking computer monitors?"

"Take it easy, there, Tim," she says coolly. "Brian's going to fix it."

"Maybe you did this on purpose." He feels the veins throb in his temples.

"Really? And why would I do that?" she says and continues to swing her feet.

"I don't know, you tell me. Maybe to sabotage the whole experiment. Maybe you have a hidden agenda." Dilly rolls her eyes, and takes another bite of her toast. He notices her diamond ring. "Maybe for the money, huh? Don't think I don't know about the clubs. I know it's you guys. I watch the news." He hobbles right up to her. "Who the hell are you, really?" Dilly holds his gaze. "And what the fuck are you doing here?" The veins on his head further bulge, and seem ready to burst.

"You're such an asshole," she says, and jumps off the counter.

Brian comes running up the stairs, laptop under his arm. "I couldn't find another power supply but—" he stops short. His right cheek twitches. "What's going on?" he asks.

Dilly is quick to answer, "Nothing, baby," she pats O'Sullivan on the arm, "Tim was telling me how much he appreciates all the hard work we've put into this."

*Not now, Tim*, O'Sullivan tells himself. *This is not the time or place to get into your brother's pathetic choice in women.*

Brian turns to his brother. "Well, thank you, Tim." He grins. "Look, we'll hook up my laptop instead for the time being," he says, and begins to set up. "Just need a couple of minutes to rewire."

Chapter 22

# BIKES DON'T GROWL

At the campsite, the students are chanting the '8 Simple Rules for Survival' while they arm for battle. Flashlights, knives, water and food are culled. Branches are carved into spears. Rocks are collected. Arrows are made.

"Check out your sister," Lance tells Billy Bob, jerking his chin in her direction.

They watch Sharon whittle the tip of her makeshift spear, chanting the rules like a child sings a song.

"Man, I must still be stoned," Lance says.

"It doesn't make sense, J.J.," Billy Bob says, his eyes still on his sister. "Why take the geeks?"

"I don't know," Jonathan answers.

"Exactly," Billy Bob tells him. "You don't."

"If the A-rab's sore at *us*," Lance says, "then why would he want to hurt *them*? The geeks didn't do anything to them".

"He's got a point, J.J.," Ronald cuts in. "We're the ones he wants, why would he—"

Heather jumps in front of Ronald. "You?" she snaps, smacking his chest. "What did you do?"

"Nothing," Jonathan says, "we were just having some fun, that's all. No reason for that fucking terrorist to do what he's doing."

"We should go find The Sarge," Lance says to all within earshot. "Or go back to the bus and get the hell out of here."

"Right," Jonathan snorts, "you have keys?"

Lance brings back his shoulders and raises his chin. "I can start the bus."

The kids drop their jaws and take a step toward Lance.

"No, not until Scott and Cindy get back," Jonathan says. "We stick together!" He cups his hands around his mouth. "Scott! Cindy!" he calls out.

"If it *is* them, and they come within a foot of us," George lunges with his spear, "I'm going to stick 'em."

"Yeah, yeah, stick 'em, stick 'em," some of the others echo, smacking their weapons against the hard ground.

"It's not them!" Billy Bob shouts.

"You heard his bike!" Jonathan counters.

"Bikes don't growl," Billy Bob argues. "And Cindy, Scott, and my sister said they heard a growl."

"But bikes *do* roar," Zack interrupts. "So maybe he popped a wheelie, flew over Scott, and kicked Cindy."

"You think everything's a fucking movie, Hollywood!" Lance shouts.

"I'm telling you it's not them," Billy Bob insists.

"Then it's got to be The Sarge," Zack affirms.

"The Sarge wouldn't kick Cindy," Billy Bob tells him. "There's something else out there," he says, his voice dropping to a whisper.

"Scott! Cindy!" Jonathan continues to call out.

A female shriek pierces the night. The group forms a tight circle and faces the woods. "Sounds like … it's coming from …" George looks around, trying to pinpoint the distant scream. "Coming from-"

"Sounds like Cindy!" Sharon cries.

Another shriek echoes. They aim their weapons and cry out: "Cindy!" The shriek gets louder, more desperate. "Cindy!" they yell again and again until they get cut off by a male screeching a primal wail in the distance.

"Scott!" Jonathan bellows. "SCOTT!"

They wait but hear nothing except the trees groaning and creaking in the wind.

"Scott!" Ronald yells.

"Cindy!"Heather shouts.

"Cindy! Jeffrey! Doris!" Sharon screams.

"Fuck this!" Jonathan heads for the woods but Lance grabs his arm.

"That's exactly what they want you to do, my brother," Lance tells him, calmly. "Like you said, *we* stick together."

"Scott's my boy, do you think I'm going to let those fuckers get away with this?" Jonathan barks, pulling his arm free.

"Do you think that Scott would have screamed like that if he ran into the A-rab?" Billy Bob cries. "No fucking way, dude. He would have capped his ass!" He points at the forest. "There's

221

something out there, but it's not The Sarge or the A-rab and his GF."

***

Jonathan lets the various possibilities sink in for a moment. He presses his hands against his face, rubs them up and down, thinking: *The Sarge, the A-rab, the GF, whatever ...* He shoots out his hands. "Whatever it is, I say we get it!"

"Yeah, yeah," George and Ronald rant. "Let's get it!"

"Get it! Get it! Get it!" the others join in, getting louder and rowdier. They point with their fingers, flay their arms, wave rocks, aim spears and arrows. Faces contorted, eyes wild, their bodies sway from left to right.

"Let's go!" Jonathan commands firmly.

"Gooooo!" they all shout.

Lance and Billy Bob hold out their arms to form a barricade and leap in front of the group.

"Will you all shut the fuck up!" Lance explodes.

The students bring down their weapons and start mumbling the Rules of Survival again.

"What's wrong with you all?" Lance belts. "What are you on? You look whacked out of fucking your minds!"

"All night you've been acting weird and crazy … and … and …" Billy Bob can't find his words.

"And horny!" Lance finishes. "Like you was in a porno."

"Yeah!" Billy Bob concurs. "Having sex like it was nothing!"

"Even Obama was getting laid," Lance says.

"And you," Billy Bob points at Zack. "You were in a threesome—"

"A foursome!" Lance exclaims. "With Dawn!"

"And she *spoke*!" Billy Bob shouts.

*She spoke?!* Jonathan repeats in his head. He looks around and notices that everything has gone silent save for the sound of pattering boots. *Eerie,* he thinks. *Unfuckingnatural.*

The group turns to Dawn. She's rocking from side to side. Mouth agape, goggle eyes staring out. *Glistening,* Jonathan notes. She holds her spear tight, raring to go.

Heather, Rosa, and Sharon stand open-mouthed and suddenly cry out in unison, "She spoke?"

"You *spoke*?" George questions.

Ronald echoes, "You *spoke*?"

"You *spoke*?" Heather asks. She pulls off one of Dawn's earphones and, over the blaring music, begs to know, "What did you say, honey?"

223

Dawn offers no response.

Heather turns to the threesome, "What did she say, Zack?"

"She said—"

A thunderous growl booms! The students jump back.

"Ronaaald!" Heather cries. But the blonde is gone before anyone can turn to her.

Ronald runs into the darkness. "Heather!" he calls out.

Another growl. Jonathan feels his shirt dampen.

"What the fuck *is* that?" Lance shouts.

"Oh my God!" Abigail shrills. "Sounds like a bear!"

Ronald screams.

George darts forward. "Ronald!"

"No! George!" Rosa charges. "Don't go!"

Lance grabs her by the hair and pulls her back into the circle, as George is also lost to the darkness.

"*Jorje!*" Rosa screeches.

"What the fuck is going on here?" Jonathan yells, watching his friends get swallowed up by the night.

A hedge ruffles nearby. Ronald staggers through it into the moonlight, one arm missing,

224

blood oozing from his mouth. He tries to speak. "You ... you ... you ... wouldn't beleeeb—" the hedge moves. A dark green blur emerges behind Ronald—as though the bush were coming to life, Jonathan thinks, horrified.

Zack points at Ronald. "Behind you! Look out!" But it's too late. Ronald is yanked back into the forest.

"Obama!" Billy Bob screams.

"Let's get the fuck out of here!" Lance pulls Rosa along. He glances over his shoulder, "Hollywood! Get the girls! Go! Go! Go! Swifty! Move it!"

"Sharon!" Billy Bob grabs his sister by the hood of her jacket. "Come on!"

"Jonathan!" Sharon shrieks, as she's being pulled. "Behind you!"

BAM! Jonathan fires a shot that echoes through the woods.

Chapter 23

# POACHERS?

O'Sullivan jerks his head up toward the window, "Did you hear that?"

"Hunters," Brian mutters, typing in commands at the laptop.

O'Sullivan wrinkles his face. "At night?"

"Poachers?" Brian raises his shoulders.

"No … no …" O'Sullivan shakes his head. "Shit. Johnson!" *That punk brought a gun!* "You've got to hurry up with that," he says, breathing down his brother's neck.

Brian hits 'Enter' and the laptop pops up four split screens, each revealing different areas of the campsite. "Like I said, poachers," he points at the images. "Everything's calm. Everything's normal."

"Where are they?"

Brian zooms in on the different areas. "The fire's burning down …," he says. "It's too dark but … nothing seems out of the ordinary." He tries to switch on the night vision mode but can't access the command from the laptop. "First thing in the morning, I'll go into Crosby and get a new power supply. You're good for tonight. They're sleeping."

"You think?" Tim asks, seemingly unconvinced.

"Brian," Dilly calls out, from the second floor.

"Or doing something else." Brian grins. "I'll be upstairs." He shoots his big brother a meaningful wink and heads for the bedroom.

O'Sullivan nods with a thin smile and turns his attention on the laptop. He focuses on each screen, switching from one camera to the next. *Puzzling*, he thinks.

***

The nine remaining students scuttle up a dense, steep hill. Lance leads with his flashlight. "Got to catch my breath," he gasps, and leans against a tree, still holding on to Rosa. He slips a beer out of

227

his pocket, cracks it open, and takes a long swig. Rosa glares at him, eyes on fire. The others stop. Some of them take out cell phones.

"There's no reception," Abigail tells them. "I've been trying all night."

"Me too," Kimberly adds, holding her phone out, lighting the dark evergreens. "Zero bars."

"When I get back home," Abigail continues, "I'm fucking changing providers."

A gusty wind ruffles the branches.

"Fucking trees are creeping me out—" Kimberly shivers "—they look alive. Like they're closing in—"

CRACK! From the woods. Jonathan's head jerks from side to side, and he points his gun. "It came from over there!"

Zack positions his bow and arrow. The other students spring back into circle formation, weapons ready, eyes fixed on the black forest. Jonathan scouts the trees. "Nothing," he states, "just the fucking wind."

Dawn stuffs her earphones back into her ears and zones out.

"Did we lose that fucking thing?" Billy Bob sputters as he gulps for air. He reaches for Lance's beer can. "Anybody get a look at what the fuck that was?" He takes a swig.

228

Jonathan looks at Billy Bob a moment and shakes his head, "No, it was too dark."

"I did," Zack says. "But you guys won't believe me."

"Don't you fucking start!" Lance warns him, pushing him out of the circle.

"But whatever it was, it was more than one," Jonathan says.

Billy Bob turns to him. "Do you think you got one?"

"I don't know," Jonathan answers. "It happened too fast."

"He missed," Lance says. "The bullet carried."

"You still think it's Elie?" Billy Bob sneers at Jonathan. "I don't think so."

"Sounded like bears," Abigail remarks, eyes wide.

"No," Kimberly counters, "sounded like wolves."

"Wolves? … There are no wolves in these parts, just coyotes," Billy Bob states.

"It *is* wolves," Sharon says. "I saw them."

"You saw them?" Billy Bob asks. "How the hell could you—"

Zack steps back into the circle. "Me too!" he cuts in. "I didn't believe my eyes, but I saw one of them stand on two feet and pull Ronald back into the woods."

Jonathan nods.

"Yeah! Yeah!" Abigail and Kimberly agree, "Me too! Me too!"

"What are you, all on fucking crack?" Lance spits out. "It was too dark to see anything. And wolves don't stand on two feet."

"They were growling," Zack says, his pupils dilated, "So if it's not wolves then it's got to be were—"

"Don't you fucking say it, Hollywood!" Lance snaps at him, fists clenched.

"I don't care what they are," Rosa cries, trying to pull away from Lance. "I say we go back and get George."

"Yeah, yeah," the group yells in agreement. "Let's go get George! Heather! Ron—"

"Shh! They're going to hear us," Lance cautions. "And close your phones … too many lights."

No one speaks for a time. Cell phones are tucked into coat pockets. The wind rattles through the trees, sending whiffs of pine and balsam.

"What if it's those crazy teens from that Club Rave On in Hope?" Billy Bob whispers. "The lady on the news said they had superhuman powers and ate some cop's ear. It's only about a half hour away from here which would explain—"

"No way teens can move that fast and sound like that," Zack says. "It's got to be wer—"

"Will you shut up with that?" Lance hisses, through gritted teeth.

"GEORGE!" Rosa bellows. "We've got to go get him!" she pleads, desperation in her voice as she turns to each of her classmates.

Lance grabs Rosa by the shoulders. "You saw what they did to Ronald! There's no way he's—"

"You guys are a bunch of chicken shits!" Rosa accuses, crying now. "I'm going myself!"

Lance tightens his grip on her arm and shakes her. "You're not going anywhere! You're staying here with us."

"George! George! George!" Rosa's screams reverberate.

"Got to be werewolves," Zack mumbles, "Could still be Elie. He looks the part, and her being from Eastern Euro—"

"Will you both shut the fuck up!" Lance erupts. "George is dead! And there's no such thing as—"

GROOOOOWL!

"Aaaaaaaaaaaaaaah!" They scream and scatter.

"Here! Over here!" Zack hollers, "Follow me!" and leads Abigail, Kimberly, and Dawn downhill.

Jonathan bolts into the woods.

"Sharon!" Billy Bob yells, as she takes off into the darkness after Jonathan.

*** 

Lance sees an opening among the trees. *This way!* he tells himself. "Go, go, go!" he orders Billy Bob. "Sharon'll be alright, J.J.'s packing." Lance scurries up the hill, pushing Billy Bob and pulling Rosa. *Gotta … get 'em … outta here!* Lance decides. He needs to save his friends.

"George!" Rosa screams, and breaks free, but in the next instant, Lance hears her foot crush a branch. A click follows, and she's swooshed upside down, ankles snared by a rope. "Jesus!" he cries. Rosa's suspended ten feet off the ground.

"What the fuck?" Billy Bob says as he and Lance watch her weapons rain down to the inclined ground below her.

"Hang on!" Lance yells up. "Shit, I'm gonna slip." He catches himself. "Swifty!" Lance holds out his hand. Billy Bob stabs his cleats into the ground, wraps an arm around a tree, and extends his spear. "Got it!" Lance shouts. He stretches his other hand up to Rosa. "Can't … reach …"

"Give me your knife!" Rosa yells.

Lance digs into his pant pocket and extends his knife. Her body sways overhead. Her fingertips graze the steel tip.

"Ouch!" she cries, nicking her finger. "Just jump, motherfucker, jump!"

Lance leaps into the air.

"Got it!" she yells.

He watches her curl her chest up against her legs and begin to slice the rope frantically.

"Hurry!" Lance begs, "Hurry!"

Rosa carves into the rope, strand by strand. "Just … one … more—" Rosa gasps. "*¿Qué coño …?*"

"What?" Lance cries.

"There's a fucking light in the tree … A red light …," she yells, slicing.

"What?" Lance hollers.

"I think it's a cameraaaaa—" The last thread snaps and she drops.

Lance lets go of the spear and holds out his arms. "I got her!" he bellows.

A dark grumbling shape streaks over him—a blast of putrid air—and Rosa is gone. Intercepted.

"Nooooooooooo!" Lance loses his footing and slides helplessly down the hill.

Rosa shrieks.

Billy Bob fishes his flashlight out of his pocket. "Rosa! Lance!"

Growl!

Billy Bob's rammed from behind; his spear and light fly. Rosa screams again. He takes out his knife. Snarls circle. "Oh, fuck … oh, fuck …," he cries. "Oh my God!" He spins on his heels and stabs into the night.

Rosa screams, "*Ayúdame!*"

GRRR!

Billy Bob faces the still imperceptible aggressor. A waft of hot vile air shoots into his nostrils. "Uggh! What the …." Rotten eggs, fish, and rusty metal. He gags at the stench, recoils, trips backwards, and falls to the ground. A sudden tug at his feet, he throws his arms out to grab at anything, and loses his knife. "Shit! Shit!" He kicks and kicks and kicks. "Let … go … of … my—" The cleats connect forcefully. A dog-like yelp pierces his ears. "Fuck you!" he screams, kicking at air— the danger has gone. *Son of a bitch!* he thinks, and realizes in the same moment that Rosa's screams have come to a halt.

Heavy footfalls race toward him. He turns and punches into the dark. A firm grip seizes his wrists mid-air.

"It's me … Lance!" Lance says, then breaks into sobs. "I had her, man … I had her …."

"Oh my God, she's gone, bro!" Billy Bob snivels. "She's gone." He leans a shaky hand on Lance's chest and bursts into tears. Lance wraps him in his arms and both boys cry.

Lance tears away from his friend and wipes his eyes. His boot steps on something solid—something that rolls. He looks down. "Rosa's spear," he says, lifting it from the leaves. He searches up at the nearest tree and points the weapon at a branch. "She said she saw a light. A camera, I think she said—" he cranes his neck "—I can't see …"

"We need to keep moving." Billy Bob slings his arm around Lance. "We need to find my sister."

Chapter 24

# WEIGHING THEIR OPTIONS

Sharon and Jonathan race through a valley, using his cell phone to light the way. Screams echo in the distance.

"Got to stop," Sharon gasps, her hand on her heart.

"Look! What's that?" Jonathan runs ten feet ahead. "There's a light up there!" He points uphill. "A cabin!" He turns to Sharon, the first signs of hope in his eyes tonight. "There's a cabin up there!"

"He's in trouble … Billy Bob … I can feel it!" she cries. "We've got to help him."

Jonathan runs back to her. "The lights are *on*! Someone's there!" he exclaims. "They must have a phone!"

***

Billy Bob and Lance stop to catch their breath and weigh options. Billy Bob is shaking his head.

"It's the only chance we've got, my brother," Lance tries to convince, "Go back to the bus, hotwire the motherfucker, and get the fuck out of hell."

"Listen to me, I don't know what they are but they hurt, bro. They hurt. I kicked one with my cleats—" Billy Bob gestures, kicking at the air "—and it ran off crying like a puppy. So we've got a shot. *You* go to the bus." He points down the line of trees that seem to slip into oblivion. "*I* need to get my sister." He takes a step in the opposite direction.

Lance places a firm hand on his shoulder. "We've got to stick together."

"No, you'll be better off on your own. You'll be able to move faster, quieter." The wind whistles. The trees sway. Fallen leaves ebb and flow. "And if you run into them, all you've got to do is yell. I'll yell back and it'll distract them. Then you can stick

237

'em." He grips Lance's spear. "But do me a favor, bro, if you don't have to, don't. Just run. Run like a motherfucker. Don't be a hero," Billy Bob's voice cracks. "If you've noticed, all the brave ones are gone."

"You know," Lance nods. He takes a moment, then says, "Alright. But take this." He hands Billy Bob his cell phone. "For the light."

Billy Bob takes it. "You make sure you come back."

"You make sure you save me some of that weed," Lance says. They grasp hands and their opposite shoulders meet.

*** 

O'Sullivan examines the screen. The camp is calm. The fire pit cradles only glowing embers and a few flickering flames. *Mesmerizing*, he thinks. Then, out of nowhere, two dark figures bound over the pit and continue off. He springs to his feet. "Brian!"

Chapter 25

# ANIMALS?

Lance runs. Spear at-the-ready, he tries to focus on his steady, heavy breathing and his imminent goal. *Will the bus start?* he wonders. *Twist the two red wires together and touch them against the brown*, he thinks, trying to recall the process. "Red, red, brown. Red, red, brown," he repeats to himself.

But no matter how loudly he shouts the words in his head, the image of his mother—wearing a red blouse—and little brother—clutching his teddy bear—flood in.

*Gotta get Moms and Lil' D outta here. Pops's gonna be fine, he lies to himself as he slips past the two thugs beating his father in the living room. He steals through his house, trying to locate his mother and brother, hoping the goons aren't drawn to his little brother's crying.*

Lance stops in his tracks, shakes his thoughts. To his left is a thick brush. *Shit.*

He turns right. Dizzy. *Where am I?*

*He hears a thug cock his gun. "Where is it? Where's my fucking money?" "I ain't got it. It's gone. I spent it," his father sputters. Lance tiptoes into the basement where his mother and Derold are crouched beside the washing machine, shielded by two stacked basketfuls of folded laundry. "Follow me," he whispers, and the three silently skulk into the garage. They open the car doors as quietly as possible; the back door creaks. Too loud, he winces. His mother ushers Derold into the second seat. Lance rips into the panel below the steering wheel—just like his father taught him. Lance can hear everything that's going on inside. "Last time! Where is it?" one of the strangers hollers. "Go fuck yourself," Lance's father curses, "You know." The thugs laugh.*

The two reds together and then the brown. *Once, twice, a gunshot booms. The engine roars.*

*Move it,* he tells himself. His legs feel like logs—deadweight. *That way to the bus.* The gunshot echoes in his head. Real? Memory? He has no idea.

*One of the goons crashes into the garage, gun raised. Lance immediately throws the car into drive and rams him into the wall. In the back, his mother and*

240

*Derold scream. Lance kicks the car into reverse, smashes through the garage door, and speeds away.*

*Here and now,* he thinks, *here and now.* He runs past his tent, over the fire pit, spear out. His throat closes up. He trips and catches himself, vomiting acidic beer; it burns as it spews out. *The bus, motherfucker, just think of the bus.* He forces one foot in front of the other. He doesn't dare stop.

\*\*\*

Brian zooms in on the frozen image on the laptop screen. His cheek twitches.

O'Sullivan leans in. "So what are they?"

"I don't know," Brian tells him, "maybe some kind of … animals? I can't make them out."

"Animals? No, they're erect."

Brian puts the image in play. He notices his fingers are trembling on the keyboard. "Humans?"

O'Sullivan glares at Brian for a long moment.

"What? What is it, Tim? *Say* it."

\*\*\*

Lance grabs on to roots, trying not to slide. *Seems impossible that I just climbed this same hill this morning,* he thinks. He reaches for a thick stem and flashes back to Rosa, dangling from the tree, reaching out to him. He remembers his first day of school when he asked Rosa which way to O'Sullivan's classroom.

241

He can recall it all so vividly.

"Who the hell you talking to?" A bulky Latino approached her as Lance carried on down the hall. A gorgeous blonde and a tall kid with an uncanny resemblance to the President checked him up and down. Most of the kids he passed smiled up at him, and whispered to one another. He passed a jock wearing a jacket with the name Johnson written across the back. "Hey, Super Star!" Lance turned, and Johnson threw him a football. Lance readied to catch the ball when a skinny kid skated over, and jumped in front of him. "Interception!" He held up his hand, "Swifty's the name." Lance high-fived him and said, "You know."

He slips his toque off to wipe the tears that flow freely down his face when the tree stem he's holding uproots. He loses his footing, grabs on to air, and tumbles down the slope for what feels like forever; landing face first in the jagged underbrush. "Jesus," he says aloud, feeling a thorny sapling stab into his neck—thankful it wasn't the spear in his hand piercing through him.

He pushes himself up and is surprised by the smoothness of a rock beneath his palm. He turns it in his hand. "A cell phone?" He almost laughs. "Light!" He pushes a button. The bars light up. "A signal! Thank you, Lord!"

"Hey!"

Lance turns.

"Hey!"

"Who dat?" Lance is in street mode, spear out, ready to kill.

"Me."

"Who?"

"Lance?"

"Hollywood?"

Lance holds out the phone. The dim light reveals Zack sitting up against a fallen tree, bow in hand, the string held taught by an arrow aimed directly at Lance.

"I got them," Zack says, and relaxes the arrow.

"You got them?" Lance darts over. "Are you sure?"

Zack nods. "I heard them drop."

"Where?" Lance asks, voice cracking—mouth so parched he can hardly speak. He spots Zack's water bottle on the ground, snatches it, and guzzles what remains.

Zack points into the trees. "There."

"Where are the girls?" Lance asks.

"I … I don't know. They screamed, then ran. They must have … must have got away."

"Which way did they go?"

243

Zack weakly points at the same trees.

"Okay, let's go find them."

"Can't. One of them got me a little."

Lance runs his light down Zack's body. His stomach is slashed open, his lower intestine hangs out. Like a slimy sausage link, Lance thinks, and feels his own stomach turn. "Shit!" Lance recoils. *Oh, God!* he thinks, "Okay. Okay. You're gonna be okay." He stabs 911 on the cell phone, but he's lost the signal. "Fuck! I'm just going to see—"

"Go seeeee," Zack slurs, "you won't beleeb …"

Lance holds out the phone for the signal. A mass—a fallen tree, he assumes—catches his eye. He turns the light on it. *Sweet Jesus! A body.* Face down with two arrows in its back. He slowly turns it around. "Abigail!" he gasps. Her tongue hangs out, blood trickles. "Oh, God! Oh, God! Oh, God!" He tries 911 again. It rings! Something gurgles to his left. He shines the light. "Kimberly!" She's propped up against a tree, an arrow through her throat. *The fucking idiot shot them!* "Hollywood! What did you do?!"

"911, what's your emergency?"

A growl roars. Zack is whisked away—*as if by a shadow*, Lance thinks. "Help us!" he screams into the phone. But the line is dead again.

244

Zack screams. Again and again. *It's coming from every direction!* "Zack!" Lance yells.

Lance takes a step toward Kimberly and stops short. The earth behind him vibrates. *Shit, the light! It'll see me!* He slips the phone into his pocket. He turns slowly. "What the fuck!" he exhales, and narrows his eyes. The pale moonlight scarcely reveals two silhouettes prowling from side to side. "Oh my God!" He feels his heartbeat hammer his chest. "Good doggie ... good doggies," he pleads.

They snarl and begin to circle him.

Lance shifts his head left to right. "Where the fuck are you? Where the fuck are you?" The snarls get closer. "Holy shit!" His rapid pulse is suffocating. His veins throb. His body jerks. *I'm going to die!*

GRRRRR!

*No!* He feels a fire course through his veins. "Come on!" he yells. He plants his feet on the ground and brings up his weapon. "You want me? Come and get me motherfuckers!"

\*\*\*

The two silhouettes—one male, one female—see Lance as though he were lit by metal-halide lamps; as brightly as if he were standing in the middle of Yankee Stadium on a Saturday night. Lance swings

245

his spear. Up, down, diagonally—like he's rowing through the air. They look for an opening.

The female scrapes her pads against the moist ground and lurks. She snarls. Lance turns to her.

The male finds Lance's counter-beat and rages. The butt of the spear connects to its ribs. A shrill howl follows. The male is thrown into a thorn bush.

The female lunges at Lance. He ducks and she jets over him. Lance swings and misses.

The male charges again. Lance turns just in time, managing to push him off. But the female attacks from behind and gashes Lance's nape. He screams, spins around, and spears her, sending her backwards. "Gotcha!"

A hair-raising growl blasts behind him. Lance smashes his elbow into the male. It howls and falls to the ground.

Lance spins and raises his weapon. "Gotcha too, mother—" The male can almost see the rest of Lance's words stay caught in his throat. "What the fuck— You? Punk bitch mother—" Lance brings down his weapon with all his strength. THUD! The spear breaks at the tip. It doesn't penetrate. "What the … fuck … *are* you?" he says, mouth agape.

"Grrrrrr." The beast bares its teeth.

A deafening shrill slices into Lance's ear as the she-beast springs across and claws Lance's face, tearing off flesh. He screams, stumbles, and drops to his knees. Both creatures circle him. They toy with their prey, taking turns cutting into him, taking pleasure in his agony.

"Is … that … all … you … got!" Lance spits blood at them.

The beasts stop to admire the red splashes, trickles, and oozing conquering Lance's smooth head. The male snarls and then digs his claws into Lance's gut while the female stabs hers into Lance's shoulders.

Lance lets out an agonized groan. "Not fair … two on one," he gurgles, "You … you know."

The female brings her paws down Lance's back as the male carves up Lance's stomach.

Lance belts out an excruciating wail that finally reaches Billy Bob's ears.

"Laaaance!" Billy Bob counters from afar.

The beasts stop mutilating Lance and turn to Billy Bob's echo.

"Swiiifty! Run! Run! It's the-Aaaaaaaaaaaaaaaaaaaaaaaaahhhhhhh!" Lance shrieks as he is sliced apart.

## Chapter 26

# GOD KNOWS WHAT YOU'VE LET LOOSE OUT THERE

"Right from the get-go you had to fuck things up, just so you could make a buck," O'Sullivan laces into Brian.

"Hey!" Brian yells, cheek twitching, "When you came crying to me four years ago and said, "Brian help me. I don't want to be a school teacher anymore. I want back in the army," I didn't say no. I was gung-ho. Because that's what brothers do for each other." He pokes a finger into his brother's chest. "But I told you this was going to take some doing. You said, "Whatever it takes, little brother." Remember?" He slams his hand on the dining table. "So, yeah … A couple of colleagues introduced me to a couple of people, and, yeah, I put it in the clubs. How else do you want to pay for all this?" Brian points at the computer, the screens, the door that leads to the lab. "On your school salary?"

Tim steps into Brian, puffs up his chest, and shouts, "You took what the old man did—"

"And made it better!" Brian shouts back, jutting out his chin. "He would've been proud of me. Unlike you, big brother, I'm no fucking patriot." They stand eye-to-eye. "I don't give a shit if the army reveres me for making super soldiers. Yeah, I'm doing it for the money. The old man died with nothing, this shithole in the woods—" He looks around the room at the old tweed couch, the moldy windowsills, and the lone light fixture that bleakly illuminates. "That's all. And you?" He points at his brother's leg. "A gimp."

O'Sullivan staggers from the blow, bows his head and says meekly, "But it's not even perfected yet. Why the hell would you put it in the nightclubs?" He stares out the window. "God knows what you've let loose out there."

249

Lead by her flashlight's beam, Dawn bolts through the forest, cheeks flushed and wild-eyed. The trees ahead rumble and she skids to a stop, holding out her spear. She quickly turns off her light. Too late. The fir branches before her are pushed apart. The pine scent overwhelmed by fetid breath stings her nostrils. She gasps. Growls echo around her. She crouches, lays down her weapon, lowers her head. And covers her eyes. They circle, sniff, poke her. Dawn remains frozen, eyes squeezed shut. Growls turn to snarls, then grunts, and then silence. She counts. *One ... two ... three ... four*. At "ten" she spreads her fingers, and breathes. *They're gone.*

***

"But you know what happens if you take too much. You know how addictive this drug is," O'Sullivan lashes. "They must have followed you."

"You're stretching, Tim." Brian wags his finger at him. "First of all, I never went near any clubs. *Dilly* ran for me."

"What kind of a woman sells drugs to kids in nightclubs?" O'Sullivan yells, the vein in his forehead visible.

"Look who's fucking talking," Brian shoots back.

"Really, Brian? What the fuck is she doing here?"

"Easy there, O'Sullivan," Brian warns, his tone low and menacing.

"What do you know about her?" O'Sullivan continues. "You met her on line. How do you know she didn't do something to sabotage the experiment?" Brian's right eye begins to twitch. "To fuck it all up so we'd chuck it and she can steal the formula? Get rich off it!"

"Hey! That's my future wife you're talking about," Brian roars, glaring at his brother. "She only went to the clubs because *I* was stuck *here*! She put her ass on the line for this experiment. So. Stop. Being. Paranoid!"

O'Sullivan starts to pace, then stops. He throws his shoulders up. "Then they must have followed her."

"Uh-uh, whatever's out there is not our doing," Brian insists.

"I know *exactly* what I gave them," Tim replies, shaking his head.

"Then I guess one of them got a hold of a little more."

"Impossible." Tim shambles over to his backpack, props it on the kitchen table and riffles through it. He counts the bottles of water

251

purification tablets, "Oh, no!" he mutters, and presses his palms to his temples.

"What?" Brian demands.

O'Sullivan is shaking. "One of the bottles is missing."

"How the fuck did you let that happen?" Brian utters, fists clutching the hair on the back of his head.

O'Sullivan's color drains. "I don't … at the stream … George …" he realizes, as the room starts to spin. "George Garcia … he made reference to …" O'Sullivan holds out the label. "Diarrhea."

"And …." Brian stands with his legs spread, arms firmly crossed.

O'Sullivan grips the table ledge. "One of the kids … must've wanted to … play a joke …." He keels over. Vomit splashes his pant legs.

"Oh, fuck!" Brian sputters, wide-eyed. "We've got to get out of here."

"No! I've got to help them," O'Sullivan stammers, and wipes his lips with the back of his hand.

"You *can't*, and you know that. *You* fucked up, O'Sullivan. Again!" Brian hammers, leaning over him. "Just like in Tikrit," he reminds.

"You said you made it better." The cold sweat travels his sunken face. "That it wouldn't happen again!" O'Sullivan blubbers.

Brian explodes, "NOT IF YOU TAKE TOO MUCH! Remember?" His whole face spasms. "Dad told you, *one* per quart. But you didn't listen. You wanted to be the hero. Downed half a bottle. You killed them all. Women, children … your own unit. And now you let *this* happen?" He points his finger at his brother's face. "It's all *your* fault!"

Something rumbles outside.

"What's that?" Brian grabs the rifle off the rack, takes a flashlight off a hook, and checks the back door window. His brother carefully pulls himself up and moves in behind him.

"You see anything?" Tim asks.

Brian stomps outside. Tim follows. The younger brother steals around the ATV, scans the periphery and lights a scattered pile of logs. "Still rolling," he says, and scans the trees. The bushes sway unnaturally from side to side. "We need to get outta here, *now*." He runs back into the cabin. "Dilly!" he hollers.

O'Sullivan chases after him. "What about my kids?" he pleads, eyes welling.

Brian stops, turns to his brother, and shakes his head. "Tikrit."

253

*No*, O'Sullivan thinks. And then he screams it.

***

Jonathan and Sharon scramble up the hill—about a hundred yards from the cabin—when she suddenly grabs her chest and falls to her knees, panting.

"What is it?" Jonathan asks.

She fixes on the nothingness before her. "Billy Bob!"

Jonathan scans the trees. "You see him? Where?"

"Here," Sharon says, tapping her head. "He's running in the woods." She watches him stop and light the way ahead. "*Shit!*" she hears him say, and sees him zigzag back the way he came. She bobs her head as though *she* were running, too. "Run! Run!" she cries.

> *Billy Bob scans the area.*

"Up!" she shouts. "Go up!"

> *He knocks his heels together, juts out the spikes, and starts uphill.*

She starts uphill.

Jonathan follows. "Where are you—"

"Look out!" she yells.

> *Billy Bob ducks.*

"On your right!" She screeches, cowering.

Jonathan drops to the ground.

254

*Billy Bob races and crests the hill.
The five bars light up on his phone.
He has reception! He dials. It rings
once, twice, three times.*

*"911, what's your emergency?"*

"Look out!" she shrieks.

Jonathan aims his gun wildly.

*A sinister roar thunders. Billy Bob
starts and loses his balance. The
phone slips out of his hand. "Shit!"
He reaches to grab it and catches
himself, rowing his arms backwards
to keep from falling—he's on the
edge of a cliff! He watches the phone
spiral down into the darkness—
"No!"—turns, and runs back into
the forest. CLICK. A net scoops him
ten feet off the ground.*

"Oh my God!" Sharon cries, tears streaming.

*He slices at the rope with his cleats.
Snarls menace beneath him. He
stops cutting ... but the net tears
open.*

Sharon screams.

*Her brother hangs by a strand.*

"Swing!" she orders.

"Sharon, what the hell is going on?" Jonathan cries.

> Billy Bob kicks at the air and
> swings, swings, letting go, flying
> through the air, reaching for the
> branch. He just misses.

"Fuck! Fuck!" Sharon curses. "He's ... he's on the ground ... it's coming! Billy Bob!"

> Billy Bob tries to take off but can't.
> One of his cleats is wedged into a
> large tree root.

"Hurry! Take it off! Hurry!" Sharon's face has gone white. Jonathan shakes her.

> Billy Bob pulls the boot off—and his
> face is simultaneously slashed. He
> tumbles down the hill.

Sharon cups her cheek and splits the air with a razoring cry. Jonathan wraps his arms around her. She shoves him hard and throws herself down the mountain.

"Sharon!" Jonathan yells, flying into pursuit.

> "Here! I'm here!" she hollers, trying to get a
> hold of her brother.
> "Sharon!" Billy Bob yells, stretching his
> hands out to his sister.
> They clutch one another; pull each
> other in, twin on twin, finally

*feeling whole. They cry fear and relief into each other's shoulders, and roll further down the incline as one. A jagged rock stabs into Billy Bob's side and he loses his grip on his sister.*

*"Nooooo!" she cries, feeling him slip from her fingers.*

*He tumbles off, ricocheting to the right. And smashes to a stop against a massive oak tree.*

"Oh my God!" she squeals, above him, over, beyond.

*"Sharon!" It is the last time her brother will breathe her name.*

Sharon continues to roll down the hill, eyes wide-open and fixed on her brother. "Nooooooo!" she wails, and watches as her brother's head is sliced clean off his neck.

Chapter 27

# YOU?

The male stands awed as he takes a moment to behold the female through his brilliant gaze. Her trim body electrifies. Her elegant fur is a silky-soft mix of dark and golden browns, accented by a long, full, magnificent tail. She holds out Billy Bob's freshly severed head, stops, and turns to look at her admirer. Her snout protrudes enough to heighten her full dark lips, flawless turned-up nose, long whiskers, and high cheekbones. Her large, pointed ears are drawn back onto her slicked back mane. She lets out a playful growl.

She bats her eyes at the male, craving his hard physique. She imagines herself pressed against his raven-black fur, embraced by his chiseled muscles, feeling as one in his warmth, his strength, his fury.

He growls back.

They playfully snarl at one another until she leans over, sets her trophy head on a stump, and drops down on all fours. The male lets out a lascivious growl. She leers at him over her shoulder, whines, and summons him with a nod. The male whines back as he approaches. He bumps against her and she bumps back. They mouth each other's powerful muzzles and touch noses as their whining grows into an eerie chant. The female arches her back and whips her tail. He circles around then mounts her, biting into her mane. He pounds into her harder and faster and their whines swell into growls that grow louder with each thrust, until she can't help but throw her head back and howl.

***

The howl echoes. Jonathan searches the night. Before him, Sharon lies lifeless, eyes bulging, head crushed into a rock. He sobs. *What the hell just happened?* he thinks. He caresses Sharon's forehead and closes her eyes. Another howl! He jumps to his feet—"Motherfuckers!"—and hurtles uphill through the woods, gripping Jeffrey's gun. "I will kill them." *Whatever* they *are*. He weaves through a thicket. *Why did Sharon act so crazy? What did she see?* he wonders, and barely manages to avoid crashing into a maple. *Why would she throw herself to her death? What's going on?* He runs faster than ever before. "Who the fuck is out here?"

BAM! He smashes into something and is thrown to the ground.

He points his flashlight. *El-Hage!* "You! I knew it!" Jonathan regains his feet, and aims his gun. A kick sends it to the ground: Alex.

"Fucking bitch!" Jonathan yells. She boots the flashlight out of his hand. Jonathan drops to the ground and feels for the gun as the pair circle him. "Terrorists! Terrorists! What have you done?" Jonathan tastes blood in his mouth. "It's your fault Sharon's dead!" he weeps.

"What?" Alex cries. "Sharon's dead?"

"And Swifty—" Jonathan pounds the ground. "What did you do to him?" Jonathan screams, still searching for the gun.

"Swifty?" Elie pants. "Nothing! Nothing! We haven't see him. We—"

"Liar!" Jonathan shouts. "You killed them! You killed them all!" He spits blood.

"Listen to me, Jonathan," Elie says, lowering his voice. "I swear to you, whatever you're thinking, it's not us."

The pair inch toward him.

*Watch them! Watch them!* Jonathan sidles. *They're lying! Don't let them get a jump on you.* "You said you were going to kill us," Jonathan cries, "and that's exactly what you've been doing all night."

"No! We came here to scare you," Alex tells him. "That's all."

"But that all changed as soon as we heard the growls and screams," Elie cries. "We got scared and took off and found a cabin …," he points at the light in the distance, "and we were about to knock … but, then we heard them … The Sarge … and his brother …"

"And we hid," Alex cries.

"Behind the logs," Elie says.

"And I slipped …" Alex snivels, "and the logs crashed—"

"And his brother," Elie continues, "came out with a rifle! So we ran."

261

"Liars!" Jonathan keeps moving. "Liars!" He pats the ground—"Liars!"—desperately searching for the gun.

"We're telling the truth!" Alex screeches. "I swear."

"The Sarge? His brother? A rifle? What the fuck are you trying to pull?" Jonathan hisses, spit flying. He starts to feel dizzy. "It was you two!"

"No! It's The Sarge!" Alex tries to convince.

"And his brother," Elie continues. "We heard The Sarge say that his brother let something loose into the woods. Those kids from the club. Super soldiers"—he takes a deep breath—"on a drug his brother created."

"You're full of shit. You heard us talking about that right before you attacked us!" Jonathan says, trying to regain his senses.

"He's experimenting on you guys, too!" Alex says.

*Don't listen to them!* Jonathan tells himself.

They move in closer.

Jonathan starts to panic. *They're going to jump you, too.* He crawls backward. Grips the earth. The twigs. The rocks. And feels the gun beneath his knee. He sweeps it up and draws a bead on Elie.

"He killed your father!" they both scream.

"And Jeffrey's!" Alex exclaims.

"He killed everybody on that mission," Elie cries. "All innocent. Women, children. His own men!"

"What? You're insane!" Jonathan shouts. "He's a hero!"

"Think about it. How incredible was that story he told us?" Elie asks. "You remember card forty-seven? We looked him up. O'Sullivan didn't kill him."

"Card forty-seven surrendered to the coalition late April," Alex says.

"The Sarge said it happened a couple of days after the toppling of Hussein's statue. That was early April. There's no way ... it was all a lie!"

"Fuck you! I know how you people work. You're trying to confuse me." He waves the gun from Elie to Alex. "Tell me the truth!" he commands, and points it at Alex's head.

"Wait! Wait!" Elie pleads. "Look at you! Tell me you don't feel different. Tell me everybody's been acting themselves tonight. Tell me you guys aren't on that fucking drug!" Streams of sweat pour off Elie's brows.

Alex gasps for air.

Jonathan squeezes his head and stares past Elie and Alex. *Could this be true?* He thinks back to the campsite: how they were all acting, how Lance

263

and Billy Bob went off on them, how Dawn looked even crazier than usual. How nothing's made any sense all night. He huffs. "We weren't afraid. We weren't afraid ... and Sharon ... Sharon *had* to be on something ... and Dawn ... Dawn *spoke*!"

"Dawn spoke?" Alex blurts.

"You see!" Elie cries, taking a step closer to Jonathan.

"Yeah, Dawn spoke ..." Realization starts to kick in. "How the fuck ... bastard!" Jonathan feels the blood rush from heart to head. He could explode. *It is true. Elie and Alex are his* allies! "Let's get him!"

"No," Elie says, "They've got a rifle."

"And I've got a gun," Jonathan counters.

"We need to get help," Alex pleads.

"He ... killed ... my ... father," Jonathan drawls as the words take shape and meaning. "He killed my father!"

"We don't know what's out here." Elie points at the forest. "My bike's in the woods," he says softly. "Alex can go get help ... there's a diner not too far from here. We'll try to find the others," he implores. "It's the best chance we've got."

Jonathan takes a long pause and breathes. Everything in his head comes together. "Okay ... okay." He pats Elie's chest. "Let's go." He grabs his water bottle with one hand, his other holds the gun. He's about to drink—"Oh, fuck! I think I get how …"

A branch snaps. Jonathan whirls and his gun goes off. Something hits the ground with a *thud*. "Elie? Elie? Alex?"

A deep-chested rumble booms behind Jonathan.

He spins around. "You? … Son of a bitch!" He fires. BANG. BANG. BANG. Another thud. He looks down. Then up.

*** 

The male beast stands before him again, relishing the terror in the young man's eyes.

"Fuck me!" Jonathan cries. "What the hell are—aaahhhhhhhh!"

The teen's chest rips open—the female beast's paw bursts out clutching Jonathan's heart. Still beating. The male places its mighty paw over hers, and together, they crush it. The female yanks her paw out—Jonathan collapses—and licks her claws. The male hops over the dead boy and dances around her, yipping and howling.

Shrubs are parted. Twigs snap. Pebbles are crushed. A light beams.

The beasts turn to look and clearly see Dawn standing tall, holding their gaze. The male bares his

265

teeth to her, then turns to his mate and points his snout toward the light in the distance: The cabin. They nod in agreement. And bolt toward it.

***

*You see,* she tells herself, *they won't hurt* you. Dawn makes her way to Jonathan. She runs the light beam over his body and angles her head. *Dead! A large hole in him!* She studies the look on his face: ... *peaceful and ... happy ... finally.* She falls to her knees. And pats Jonathan down. Rummages through his pockets. She tugs the inside coat pocket—*What's this?* A bottle of Water Purification Tablets. She suddenly recalls when they were at the stream: the shifty look on Jonathan's face when his gloved hand reached into O'Sullivan's backpack and stole a bottle of tablets. She yanks it out and shakes it. *Empty!* She flings it.

*Where is it?* She flashes her light. *There it is!* Jonathan's water bottle gripped tight in his lifeless hand. She pries it free—one finger at a time. Pops it open and guzzles it down.

## Chapter 28

# GOT TO GET THE FUCK OUT

Brian races up from the basement carrying a heavy cardboard box full of beakers, burners, and flasks. He heads for his jeep out front.

Dilly's black leather boots clump noisily as she runs down the stairs, tucking in her shirt. She twists her hair into a messy bun and zips up her jacket.

"Get my laptop," Brian yells from outside.

Tim is at a standstill, watching. *He's abandoning*, he thinks. *Our experiment … it's dead.*

Dilly rushes over to the dining table, snatches the laptop, and runs out. "Almost forgot."

O'Sullivan grabs the flashlight and heads for the back door.

Brian hurries back in. "Tim, what are you doing?"

He half turns, and looks back at his brother. "Got to get my kids."

"No, *we've* got to go."

"I can't desert them!"

Brian grabs the rifle. "You heard the shots—" he pulls back the bolt handle "—the screams?—" and checks the chamber. He pushes the handle forward and locks it down. "They're. Not. Your. Kids. Anymore!"

"I can't leave until I know for sure. How am I going to explain this?" He slumps and appears much smaller than his uniform.

"You can't, big brother. There's no cover-up this time. No hero stories, no medals. We've got to get the fuck out. Come on!" Brian pulls on his brother's sleeve.

"Brian! Come on!" Dilly calls from outside. "Let's go!"

"You said you were going to help me with this." O'Sullivan struggles to break free from his brother. "You promised."

268

Brian grabs him by his jacket collar and pins him against the door. "Either you come with me now or I'm going to leave your crippled ass here so your fuck ups can have a go at you."

Dilly rushes back in. "Brian, come—

\*\*\*

Her mouth widens. She points at something behind Tim—at the back door. "Ahhhhhhhh!" she screams. The door crashes into O'Sullivan and sends him smashing into Brian. The gun goes off and shoots the light overhead. It's dark save for the rolling flashlight on the floor. Both men are down.

Dilly cries, "Oh my God, Brian! Oh my God!" Suddenly she's being snarled at, circled, and backed into a corner. "Tim! Help me!"

Brian shakes himself out of his daze, finds the rifle—

"No!" O'Sullivan jumps on top of Brian but he is no match for his younger brother. Brian whacks O'Sullivan's head with the rifle butt and knocks him out.

GROWL!

Dilly screams. Brian opens fire. An abominable shrill rattles the cabin and Dilly darts out the back door. She trips over a scattered log and is sent sprawling to the ground—bashing her cheek into another piece of firewood. She pushes

269

herself up—*The four-wheeler! Keys!*—leaps to her feet, jumps on the ATV, and turns the key already in the ignition. "Brian!" she yells and revs the engine. A spatter of thick blood sails toward her. Something pelts her side. She looks. Brian's bloody, severed head sits sideways in the mud. Eyes out of their sockets. Dangling. Mouth twisted open. Trachea hanging out. She screams. The bike's front wheels fly into the air and the vehicle flips over. She is thrown backwards down the mountainside. She slides, rolls, and smashes to a stop. *Fuck!* she rubs her shoulder, *hurts*. She moans, and automatically begins patting the ground around her. "What is … this?" Something is sticking to her fingers. She manages to turn her head and look. A body. *No*, a corpse. Long, ginger hair. *The twin! Oh, my God!* She jumps to her feet.

***

Wet. Slimy. Slobber. O'Sullivan begins to regain consciousness and automatically wipes the saliva dribbling down on his face. He blinks, and tries to catch his breath. His brother. That is his brother. Or *was*, he thinks, eyeing the scattered remains. Thick gobs of drool smack his cheek. He turns his head and gasps. Snarls—inches from his face. "Listen to me. I'm sorry. I never meant for it to get to this. I know what you're going through."

GROWL!

"I've been there! Don't let it take over you. You can control it. You need to reach insiiiiiiiiiiiiiiiiiiiiide!"

Blood gushes. A dull throbbing begins at his legs. It grows in intensity and the pain begins to overtake his senses. He is being torn apart. Panic sets in. "Aaaaaahhhh!" he wails. He begins to tremble and shake. His gimp leg is sliced off, held up, and bitten into. The bullet lodged in the leg is spat out at him. The Sarge begins to laugh—loud and uncontrollably. He reaches for the slug and squeezes it tight. "I ... always ... knew ... you'd make great ... soldiers!" he groans. "Come on ... finish me off!" he orders. "Hoo-ahhhh!"

*\*\**

Dilly cuts through the woods. *Far away,* she thinks. *Get as far away from here as possible.* She feels a splinter in her cheek, but there's no time for that now. *Why did Brian have to go back in? Why didn't he just leave his brother? We could've been in the pick-up or on my bike ... away from here ... safe. Brian ....* She sobs. Her legs feel heavy. Her feet like lead blocks. She trips and falls. Feels around. *Not a log.* She focuses. Another body. *Scott, the stunning boy on the bus!* He's dead. Genitals ripped out. She covers her mouth to mute a scream, crawls backwards and

271

bumps into another body. A girl. The Asian with the platinum hair … *Cindy*. She lies chest down, her head is twisted around, facing up.

Dilly presses both hands against her mouth, jumps to her feet, and hobbles over fallen branches, twisted shrubs. Then: *Fuck!* She's stepped into a trapping pit—camouflaged in a weave of dry cattails that she made herself. She yells in her head as she reaches one hand out mid-air and grabs on to a loose tree root. Her body smashes against the pit's inner wall but she manages to hang on. She tries to pull herself up. "Oww," *my shoulder*. She catches sight of a hand reaching out to her from the lip of the hole. *Oh, thank God!* She grabs it. Ronald's severed arm slides into the pit, as Dilly falls to the trap's bottom.

The landing is soft. She feels beneath her. Damp. Lumpy. *Animal?* A faint light glows. She fumbles for it. *Coat?* Her fingers slide under wet shredded serge. She wrenches out a flashlight. *Oh, God.* The mutilated bodies of three more. Heather … Ronald … and another boy, she can't be sure— the blood, the carnage. She lets out a scream that rips through the mountains. Then faints.

***

Dilly opens her eyes. *Where am I? … Shit!* she scrambles to her feet and jumps, but the ledge is too high. She begins to tremble. Bodies heaped around her—the stench of blood and death. It's choking. The bodies ... *yes!* She bites down on the flashlight and rolls—*George, that's right, George!*—against the wall. Though heavy, she hauls Ronald by his one arm and struggles to lift him on top of George. Heather is too blood-soaked to roll, so Dilly grabs her by the hair and pulls. The head starts to dislodge. "Sorry! Sorry!" She sets it down gently and grabs for boots instead. Dilly drags her next to the boys, unzips Heather's jacket to get a better grip, and uses George's pants to wipe the blood off her hands. She slides them behind Heather's back and heaves her on top of Ronald. *Fuck!* Heather's head pulls more apart. It dangles to the side, held on by a carotid artery.

Dilly steps on Ronald's remains and pulls herself up. Heather's ribs crack under the weight. The bodies wobble beneath. The once pretty blonde head snaps off. Dilly jumps and gets a hold of the ledge. "Owww!" Her flashlight slips out of her mouth. *Fucking shoulder!* She scrabbles over the rim—*I made it!*—gets to her feet, takes a painful step forward. And feels a firm grip on her shoulder.

A mass of rancid hotness courses down her neck. She whips around, and smashes what's in front of her into the pit.

Dilly runs.

Chapter 29

# BACK TO THE ENDING

Crosby is a small town. Quiet. Its people are pleasant, but prefer to keep to themselves. The few shops there never stay open past six o'clock, except, for the Eats All Nite diner, an old fueling station that stands alone in a vast parking lot on the outskirts. The diner honors its name. The gas pumps have been dry for a few years now, but many truckers still make a point to stop over for Old Man Sam's filling meals, topped with his famously delectable brownie. Samuel Burton's wife, Maggie—gone two years now—won many a Blue Ribbon for those.

Currently, Sam balances a white plate, featuring a large chocolate brownie, topped with whipped cream, hot fudge, chocolate sprinkles and a plump maraschino cherry. He passes a young couple, Kurt and Annie, who sit in a booth and follow the dessert plate with their eyes. He sets the plate down in front of Gary—a clean-cut truck driver. Sam sniffs the air. "You hauling fish again this week, eh, Gary?" he says, wrinkling his nose. His upper denture shifts and he repositions it with his tongue.

"Enjoy!" Annie tells Gary from the next booth.

Gary looks up at the couple and frowns. "You'd better believe I'm going to enjoy this," he says, waving his fork, "'cause I work hard for my money. I pay my taxes and have never taken a dime from anybody. Saved up and paid for my rig out there *cash*" —he points out the diner's rail car style window— "and nobody's going to take that away from me," he opens his jacket to reveal a gun in its holster. "That's why I carry this baby," he says, and pats his weapon.

Speechless, the couple turn to each other and sink back into their seats.

Gary tugs his baseball cap down lower, *Live Free or Die*, blazoned in gold letters across it. He tucks his napkin into his collar, and is about to dive into his dessert, when the suspended television in the room's corner attracts his eye. "Turn it up. Turn it up!" he demands.

Old Man Sam starts and turns up the volume. "Hey, isn't that your trucker buddy, Drew?"

"Shhhhh." Gary jumps out of his seat.

> "Mr. Daniels, what happened out there?" the reporter on TV asks.
>
> Drew shrugs and raises his palms.
>
> "What happened to your passenger?"
>
> "They must have taken her," Drew responds, rubbing the back of his neck.
>
> "Who? Who has taken her?"
>
> "I ah … I don't …"
>
> "Mr. Daniels, what is out there?"
>
> "I don't know. But whatever it is, you come across it … you'd better run for your life."

The bells on the diner door ring as it swings open. The blaring hum of Gary's reefered trailer greets the diners. Everyone looks. Jeffrey and Doris stand at the doorway: mud-covered, lacerated, bloody. Their clothes are torn into strips, their chests shielded by bulletproof vests—sheathing two bayonets, each. Hand on her hips, Doris's left arm is caked with blood, her nails are broken, the skin peeled off her knuckles; scabbing. Bruised wrists are stained with dried blood from beneath her barbed bracelets. Half an arrow protrudes from Jeffrey's back. Crustlike lesions speckle the right side of his face.

***

"Jesus, Mary, and Joseph!" Sam exclaims. The boy's nose is busted, he notices. Eyes bloodshot, swollen, and bruised. Three distinct dents mark his gashed vest. *Bullets*, Sam thinks. *Bullets that bounced right off.*

***

Elie trudges through the forest, croaking for help. He carries a whimpering Alex. Her stomach bleeds; it caught Jonathan's accidental shot. "We can make it," he says hoarsely. "The road up ahead … have to get there before the troopers … take off." Both teens keep their sights on the flashing red and blue car lights.

278

Trooper Anderson peels off down the road. Trooper Valenza is about to get into his vehicle when he hears branches snap among the trees. He flashes his light, but can't make anything out in the thick darkness. He crosses the road, unclips his gun—for the first time in his three years on the force—and holds it out, flashlight pointing. "Who's there? Who's there! … What the hell am I doing?" He runs back to his car. A raspy, "Hey! Hey!" forces him to turn around.

***

Elie stumbles shakily toward him. *I saved her*, he thinks. *Alex is going to be okay.* "Officer! Officer!" he cries out.

"Jesus! What the hell happened to you guys?" Trooper Valenza takes the limp, injured girl in his arms. The second he does, the boy collapses.

***

Jeffrey and Doris lean against the counter, glued to the news report on the television.

"I said, what the hell happened to you?" Gary demands. When the kids don't respond, he turns briefly to Kurt and Annie, "This is what I'm talking about." Gary digs his bony fingers into Jeffrey's shoulder and turns him around. "Hey, I'm talking to you, punk."

Doris slinks behind Gary as Jeffrey unsheathes two blood-stained bayonets. The man stares at the ten-inch blades. He draws his gun, and aims it at Jeffrey's head. Jeffrey belts out a ferocious growl. "Not impressed," Gary says, and cocks the hammer.

Jeffrey looks past Gary and nods.

The trucker raises a brow and turns. The girl's bayonet comes across. He squeezes the trigger—"Shit!"—the safety is on. The blade slices across his neck. Blood sprays the windows and walls. He crumbles to his knees. The last thing he sees is the girl's bloodshot scowl; last thing he hears is her barking.

***

Doris yips and yowls as she watches the male werewolf pounce and swing his claws across the man. She drops on all fours and crawls toward them. She bites into the man's hand, pulling, tearing, digging in her canines as the he-wolf rips the arm off, spattering blood everywhere.

A US Army commercial tries to inspire. Jeffrey whips Gary's severed arm toward the images. Crouched behind the counter, Old Man Sam sprints out of the way as the television crashes to the linoleum. He slips on a blood pool and smashes the back of his head against the floor. Kurt and Annie take cover under their table.

***

The parking lot at the Eats All Nite diner teems with emergency vehicles. The diner's windows are obscured by drawn shades and blood. Deputies and troopers point guns at every angle. Emergency personnel stand by. Behind the blockade, reporters wait on the biggest story of their careers. Gary's reefer blares.

Trooper Anderson peers through binoculars. "I can't see anything," he tells the Sheriff, next to him.

"I'm calling inside," the Sheriff says nervously. He sets his own binoculars down on his car hood and punches in the diner's number. He points at Gary's reefer. "Turn that blasted thing off!" he orders a rookie deputy.

A black SWAT van pulls into the lot. A team of four—fully armed—and their Commander circle and position themselves around the establishment.

***

Doris and Jeffrey laugh and squeal. Doris bites into Gary's severed head and tosses it to Jeffrey. They toss it back and forth and toy with the rest of Gary's body parts like pups with bones; flinging them about, incidentally spraying the walls and

281

windows with more blood. They bark, paw at each other, and wrestle. They tumble and Jeffrey lands on top of Doris. He starts to lick the blood off her snout when the phone rings. And rings. The hum of the noisy trailer has stopped. They creep towards the entrance and Doris clears a streak off the bloody window.

***

Trooper Valenza presses a bandage over Alex's wound. She lies in the back seat of his car, semi-conscious. Elie, gasping for air in the front, tries to regain control of his shuddering limbs. *My ribs must be broken*, he thinks. *Why else would it hurt so much to breathe?* Sirens approach. Elie opens the water bottle Trooper Valenza handed him and sips slowly. "It was an accident," Elie wheezes. "I think—no, I'm sure … he got startled … then growling … moaning … animalistic …. It was dark. He fired three shots … *three* … he went down … but got right back up again."

"Are you sure?" the trooper asks.

"Yes, sir," he says. "How is that possible?"

Valenza pulls out his phone and dials.

Elie glances over at Alex, and sobs. "Is she going to be alright, sir?" An ambulance pulls up behind them, followed by another trooper car and a news van.

282

***

The SWAT Commander marches up to the Sheriff. "What do we got, Hank?"

"So far, nothing," the Sheriff says, holding up his phone, "they won't pick up."

Trooper Anderson's phone rings. "Anderson," he answers.

The Commander pats Hank on the arm and bustles over to his two sharpshooters, who each position and load their sniper rifles on the hood of the Sheriff's car. "What do we got?" he asks them.

"It's a goddamned mess, Commander," replies the veteran sharpshooter, peering in through his night vision riflescope. "One's barely moving, two others are motionless but appear to be alive, one's scattered all over the fucking place, or maybe it's two, and two—"

Trooper Anderson dashes over, hollering, "You need to hear this!" He hands the SWAT Commander his phone. "It's Trooper Valenza."

"Go ahead," the Commander says into the receiver. He listens. His forehead creases, and he nods. "Copy that." He hands Anderson back his phone, goes into the utility pack, and takes out a pair of night vision binoculars. "I'll get an eye inside the diner now," he says. The others freeze. The leader focuses, then: "Shit!" He digs back into

283

the pack and takes out a box of ammunition. "Here," he orders the marksmen, handing them each silver tipped bullets.

"Commander?" They both say with the same questioning look on their faces.

"They're wearing body armor," he explains.

"I didn't see that, Commander," the younger marksman says.

"How could you?" The Commander answers, pointing at the blanketed bloodstained windows. "On my mark," he orders, lifting his hand.

The sharpshooters unload and reload in a flash. The Commander signals the other team members.

The sharpshooters take aim.

*\*\*\**

The teens crawl to the rear door—knives in hand—but hear voices beyond the walls. They draw back and begin to circle the diner.

Kurt and Annie are huddled under the table along the front wall. "They're g-g-going t-t-to kill us, t-too," Annie whimpers to her boyfriend. "You-you-you-you've got to … d-d-do something—"

The ragged teens turn sharply to her. Jeffrey lets out a low, guttural snarl.

Annie winces.

Kurt meets the boy's piercing gaze.

Jeffrey bares his teeth, mouth frothing.

Annie grabs at her chest. She opens her mouth as if to speak but begins to gasp uncontrollably.

"Annie!" Kurt cries, shaking his girlfriend. "Annie!" He steals a glance at the gun on the floor and dives for it.

Jeffrey and Doris release powerful growls and spring at the couple.

CRASH!

Two armor-piercing bullets burst through the window.

Doris smashes to the ground, pelted by the spray of shattered glass. Jeffrey bashes into a chair and lands face-first next to her. He tries to pull himself up but his forearms slip on the tiny bits of blood-drenched window. He takes in Doris; tilts his head at the hundreds of tiny glass shards that stab into her, frowns at the hole in her chest. He looks down at his own chest. His elbows give way.

The SWAT members charge in. "Clear!" they yell from opposite sides of the diner.

The Commander, Sheriff, Trooper Anderson, and deputies pour in.

"My God!" the rookie deputy gasps, stepping into the bloodbath.

The Commander runs his eyes over the carnage and spots a young man rocking a near-hysterics young woman in his arms under a table, and Old Man Sam on the ground. "Get a medic!" he yells, then slams his boot over Jeffrey's right hand and points his rifle at him. The team members aim their weapons at Doris.

The Commander kicks the bayonet out of Jeffrey's hand with his heel, then, with the toe of his boot, rolls the boy onto his back. "Bingo!" says the Commander. "You got him right through the heart."

The rookie doubles over and vomits.

"Get him out of here!" the Sheriff hollers.

"Jesus Christ," Anderson mumbles, eyeing the downed perpetrators. "They're kids."

"They're killers, Trooper," the Commander declares, and crouches down to check Jeffrey's vitals. "Dead," the Commander affirms, and leans over Doris. He studies her carefully then looks back at Jeffrey. "Are these two the ones who attacked the club in Hope?"

"No, Commander," Anderson answers. "Valenza said they're part of the school kids up here on a weekend survival trip."

"Hmm," the Commander mutters, unconvinced. "Their wounds look about a week old."

Doris takes a short breath.

The Commander jumps back and points his weapon. "Freeze!"

***

Doris turns to Jeffrey. *My beautiful werewolf ... dead.* She whimpers and howls softly.

"Medic!" the Commander shouts.

Doris turns to the man in camouflage and tactical gear. "I always ... knew ..." she mutters to the Commander, "you'd come back ... for me ..."

The medic undoes her vest.

"Don't worry about me ...," she mumbles, smiling up at the Commander. "Everything's ... gonna be ... hunky-Doris, Dad ... dy." The lights in her eyes flash out, and she is still.

"Sweet Jesus ..." the Sheriff shakes his head. "In all my years ...."

***

"Tragedy has hit small town America once again," Anita Hemsley says into the camera. She's standing in front of the diner, her mike at chin level.

Behind the barricade, the townspeople cry and cling to one another. A German Shepherd strains at its collar and howls at the scene. A modern RV rolls slowly by—husband, mother, and two teen daughters stare from the windows. Above, a helicopter can be heard approaching from the south. Reporters are held back as they try to push their way into the diner.

"It's pandemonium here," Anita says. Behind her, officers dart back and forth between emergency vehicles and the diner. Old Man Sam is wheeled into an ambulance. Reporters besiege the blood-soaked young couple as they are brought outside, arms tightly holding each other. They approach their Mazda and Kurt fumbles in his pocket for the key.

"Where do you think you're going?" An officer takes him by the elbow and leads the dazed pair toward an ambulance.

\*\*\*

Warren and Olivia sit in their living room watching the special news report.

> "Two teenagers in army fatigues and bulletproof vests butchered a man with large knives and injured another at the Eats All Nite diner in Crosby tonight. The Sheriff's department and SWAT team were called to the scene and had to act quickly. Both perpetrators have reportedly been shot and killed. Witnesses say the male and female behaved

like rabid dogs. The slaughter may or may not be linked to incidents reported along the East Coast in recent weeks, where it was discovered that a powerful hallucinogen was being passed off as the drug Ecstasy—"

Anita stops, presses two fingers to her ear, and listens for a long moment.

"This just in: it seems the perpetrators, often victims of bullying, are part of a group of Hopper High School students on a weekend survival trip."

Warren's first to his feet. "Jesus Christ!"

Olivia keeps pace as they fly up the stairs, leaving the television blaring to an empty room.

"Police came upon a male and female student on Highway thirteen not far from where the class had been camping. The boy's extreme heroics saved his classmate's life after she was accidentally shot by one of the others. One moment, please—"

She listens into her earpiece.

"The teen claims that their teacher secretly experimented on his students, testing a powerful drug causing some to be extremely dangerous. Police are combing the woods for the rest of the class."

Olivia bursts into Jeffrey's bedroom.

Warren storms the master bedroom, throws the closet door open, and pushes his suits out of the way. "Oh, my God! It's unlatched!" He slides the hidden door open. "Jesus! They took the armor and weapons! Olivia!" he yells. "They took everything!"

"Warren!" Olivia cries back, and runs toward his voice. She holds out a pair of drawings, and shoves the first toward his face. "This one is signed by Doris."

Warren sees a female werewolf offering a severed head. "And that's Jeffrey's," he says, of the other detailed sketch: a male werewolf biting into a man's severed leg. An abandoned cane is scarcely visible in the page's bottom corner. Warren says it first: "That's … that's … O'Su—"

"Ohhhhhhhh, Jeffrey!" Olivia's legs wobble, and she sways into Warren, but drops before he can catch her.

Chapter 30

# ME TOO, ME TOO!

A light beam bounces across the cabin floor. Body parts, legs, and arms, hang and lean, *like sick decorations*. The light finds O'Sullivan, limbless, except for his right arm. He is gripping the kitchen table leg, trying to shake his backpack off. He turns to the flashlight's beam, blocking the ray with his palm.

"Evans? … Evans! Dawn, help me … please," he begs. "In … in my … backpack …"

*His backpack!*

"My gun …" O'Sullivan cries. "I …"

Dawn rips the backpack apart and extracts a bottle of water purification tablets. She takes a moment to feel its weight and spies The Sarge's canteen on a chair. *Just like Jeffrey's.* Her eyes light up. She flashes back to sitting around the campfire—when Jonathan frowned at her and held a finger to his lips after he laid Jeffrey's canteen down behind him. *That's it!* she figures, *He poured all the pills in his water. That's why they're like that.* She tears open the bottle in her hand. *Me too, me too.*

O'Sullivan gasps. "What are … you doing?"

Dawn brings the bottle to her mouth and tilts her head back.

"No, Dawn, no!"

She downs the contents and guzzles his water.

"You don't … want to … end up … like … Jeffrey and Doris!"

Dawn's hand flies up to cover her eyes, but she stops herself. She examines her fingers, sensing a current surge through them. Feeling power electrify her entire body. *Yes!* She slings O'Sullivan's backpack over her shoulder and proceeds to the front door.

"Dawwwwn!" O'Sullivan cries.

A moan escapes her. She hesitates by the door, and turns to the mirror beside it. She holds her flashlight beneath her face: sunken skin, charred flesh, hollow eyes. *Awesome!* She pulls off her earphones, flashes her teeth, and groans at the zombie in the mirror.

O'Sullivan whimpers. She turns to him.

**THE END**

# ACKNOWLEDGEMENTS

First and foremost, we'd like to thank our editor, Shelley A. Leedahl, whose relentless "Work harder!", "Remember whose POV you're in!" and "ha! ha!" in the margins not only pushed us to go way beyond our own expectations but taught us a hell of a lot about narration. Special thanks to our Beta reader, Jenny Robson, for foregoing sleep on our behalf. To Diego Briceño Orduz and Dominic James for their invaluable input on the screenplay. Sandy Martinez, Brenda Sawyer and Argiris Vamvas for their time and energy. Jacek Stomal for designing the screenplay's website. Emmanouil Vamvas at MV CPA Inc., who not only counts our cents, but takes the time to give us his two. And to Victor Malarek, for supporting two people he doesn't even know.

Heartfelt thanks to our mentor, William (Bill) Mastrosimone. We called him over twenty years ago to thank him for writing such a beautiful play (The Woolgatherer). We asked if he had another two-hander we could tour. He said, "No. Why don't you write one yourselves?" He's been supporting us ever since. Thanks, Bill.

# A NOTE FROM THE WRITERS

The core idea and title for WHEREWOLVES came to us over ten years ago. As lifelong horror film fans, it was especially the likes of George Romero's realistic treatment of the horror-thriller *Martin* that left a lasting impression on us. We knew that if and when we wrote WHEREWOLVES, it could only happen if the story were realistic; that the events could actually happen. Life went on but we continued to gather and store bits and pieces of real-life stories and events. We were especially marked when a young Canadian soldier, who, knowing we were writers, pulled us aside in a department store. He divulged he was certain his food had been drugged by the military to make him and his unit exceedingly aggressive during a peacekeeping mission overseas. Back many months, the young man felt betrayed, violated, still traumatized by what had happened there. "They did shit to me, bro. All kinds of shit. They made me do things that I can't ever repeat. You gotta write something about this. But don't tell them it was me." Whether what he told us was truth or imagined, that encounter gave us the edge for WHEREWOLVES.

WHEREWOLVES is not so much a horror story as it is a social commentary. The story is a reflection on how 'the road to hell is paved with good intentions'. It looks at parents who serve their country, but at great cost to their kids. Teachers who mean well but are riddled with their own monsters. Political events that have skewed our views of the world. Peer pressure, greed, insecurity, desensitization, ..., it goes on. Despite their lack of likability, we hope our characters' humanity shines through, thus distorting the reader's concept of good and bad, black and white, right and wrong. To us, the horror of the story is not the monsters, but how monstrously we are capable of treating one another.

# ABOUT JOHN VAMVAS AND OLGA MONTES

"BANG-ON DIALOGUE.
Vamvas and Montes make
it look, sound, smell real."
–*The Edmonton Journal*

"IMPRESSIVE TALENT
in this
writing/producing/acting
team." –*The Winnipeg
Free Press*

John Vamvas and Olga Montes in *Sarpedecinnente*

"Montes and Vamvas continue to demonstrate their skills
with SWITCHBLADE-SHARP EARS FOR DIALOGUE
and hard, thoroughly believable plot lines." –*The Sunday
Journal*

"A SEXY and EXPLOSIVE style that pulls the patrons
forward to the edge of their seats." –*The Edmonton
Journal*

Olga Montes and John Vamvas in *Bad Boy*

"RAZOR-SHARP LINES" –
*SEE Magazine*

"Montes and Vamvas are
known for their journeys
into the dark corners of the
human soul ...
EXCEPTIONAL. One of the
BEST SHOWS of the
Festival." –*Robert Enright,
CBC, Arts Tonight*

297

Together for over 20 years, John and Olga started as an acting team but soon began to write their own scripts for lack of finding two-person plays they could tour across North America. They wrote and toured four full-length critically acclaimed plays to packed houses across Canada and the United States, including, *Bad Boy*, which they performed Off-Off-Broadway at New York's Creative Place Theatre in the heart of Times Square.

In 2001, they were approached to star in and co-write the short film, *Things Never Said in Playa Perdida*. *Playa* won the audience award at the New York Short Film Festival in 2002 and tied first place at the Festivalisimo festival in Montreal.

WHEREWOLVES was written as a screenplay in 2010. They wrote the novel to get the story out while they wait for it to hit the screens.

www.ingramcontent.com/pod-product-compliance
Lightning Source LLC
Chambersburg PA
CBHW060851250626
47159CB00008B/2695